FOLLYFOOT

MONICA DICKENS

FOLLYFOOT

HEINEMANN : LONDON

William Heinemann Ltd
Michelin House
81 Fulham Road
London SW3 6RB
LONDON MELBOURNE AUCKLAND

First published 1971
Reprinted 1988

0 434 93463 1

Printed in Great Britain by
Richard Clay Ltd
Bungay, Suffolk

I

On these early spring Sundays, there were usually a few visitors who came to the farm at the top of the hill.

Some of them were regulars, horse-lovers and children with carrots and apples and sugar for all the horses, and special snacks for their favourites. Peppermints for Cobbler's Dream. Soft stale biscuits for Lancelot, who was too old to have much use of his teeth.

Some of the people who came into the yard under the stone archway were strangers who had been driving by, saw the sign, 'Home of Rest for Horses', and stopped to see what it was all about.

'What's it all about then?' The two boys who had roared up on a motorbike were not the sort of people who usually came to the farm. Nothing much doing here. Daft really, the whole outfit. 'What's it all about?' The taller boy swaggered across the yard as if he had come to buy the place: cracked leather jacket with half the studs fallen out, cheap shiny boots, long seaweed hair, a scrubby fringe of beard that wouldn't grow.

'Saving lives,' Steve muttered, not loud enough for them to understand. They wouldn't understand anyway, that kind. Steve went on sweeping the cobbles, his head down, dark hair falling into his eyes.

'Huh?' The shorter, thicker boy looked as if his mother should have had his adenoids out long ago.

'Horses that are too old to work, or too badly treated – we give them a good life.'

'Daft, innit?' The boys went jeering towards the loose boxes that lined three sides of the yard.

'Willy. Spot. Ranger. Wonderboy.' The younger boy, about sixteen, with a stupid hanging lip, spelled out the names above the stable doors, to show he could read. 'Cobles Dram. Whoever heard of a name like that?'

'Cobbler's Dream.' Callie came out of the stable, where she had been brushing the mud off the chestnut pony, whose favourite rolling places would delight a hippopotamus. 'And everybody's heard of him. He was on television. He was in all the newspapers for catching a horse thief.'

'Thrills.' When the boy hung his big cropped head and looked up at her with his slow eyes, she thought for a moment she knew him. Where had she seen that broad earthy face with the thick lips hanging open, because he could not breathe through his pudgy nose?

One of the boys threw up a hand and the pony flicked back his ears and jerked his head away.

'That's not the way to go up to a horse,' Callie said. 'Especially Cobby. He's half blind.'

'Don't tell me about horses,' the boy grunted. 'We've got dozens of 'em at home.'

'Bad luck on *them*.' Usually Callie was polite to the visitors. Her mother was married to the Colonel, who ran this farm, and Callie loved to take people round the stables or down the muddy track to the fields, and tell them the history of each of the twenty horses, or as much as they would listen to.

But these boys would not listen to any of it. When she started to tell them about Wonderboy, who had been her father's famous steeplechaser before he died, and Ranger with the ruined mouth, and Spot, the circus rosinback with the rump as broad as a table, the taller boy said, 'Oh shut up, you silly kid,' and the younger one stuck out a boot and tripped Callie up as she turned to go on to the mule's box.

'What the hell are you playing at?' Steve was there in

seconds, holding the broom like a weapon, his clear blue eyes hard with anger.

'Don't touch me,' the boy whined, 'or I'll call the coppers.'

'I'll call them myself if you don't get out of here.'

'Can't wait,' the older boy said. ' "Visitors Welcome", it says on the sign. Some welcome. Come on, Lewis.'

Willy the mule stared sadly over his door, a pocket of air in his lower lip, lop ears sagging. Callie, inspecting her grazed hands for blood and disappointed to find none, yelled after them as they ran under the arch, 'Don't bother to come back!'

'Don't worry!' Lewis yelled back over his shoulder. Yes... there was something familiar about him. Where on earth – ?

'Lewis.' She wiped off her hands on the seat of her patched jeans, as if she were wiping off the disgustingness of Lewis.

'Louse,' Steve said.

The motorbike snarled, spat foul smoke and roared away.

2

Dora, the girl who worked with Steve in the stables, had been home for the weekend, but she came back on an early bus, to help with the feeds. She would rather be here than at home anyway. The Colonel had to force her to take an occasional weekend at her parents' flat in the industrial town which sprawled along the valley, to keep her mother from storming up the hill to complain.

Steve's mother did not come, and he had no father. This was his home, and his family. Cobbler's Dream, the pony he had rescued from a spoiled and vicious child, was the horse he loved best.

It was going to be a wet night, so Dora brought the rest of the old horses in from the fields. She was coming round the corner of the barn with the two Shetlands, a handful of shaggy mane in each hand, when a car stopped in the road and a man walked into the yard. A worn-looking horsey type of man, with bow legs and a lean brown face.

'I'm sorry, we're closed to visitors.' Dora shoved one Shetland into its stable with a slap on its bustling bottom, and made a grab for the long tangled tail of the other, as it ducked under her arm and headed for the feed shed. 'Shut that door!'

The man moved quickly and shut the door in Jock's square face. Dora got her arms round his neck and practically carried him back to the loose box he shared with Jamie and the tiny donkey. They had tubs on the floor because the manger was too high, and they nipped each other round and round the box, going from tub to tub like a buffet lunch.

'I've come to see the manager,' the bow-legged man said.

'The Colonel?' You were supposed to say he was not at home on Sunday afternoons, but Dora always stated facts, even when they were ruder. 'He's in the house, but he can't see you.'

'Why not?'

'He's probably asleep.'

The man bit his lip, which was cracked and dry, like badly kept leather. 'Could you possibly. . . . It's an emergency. About a horse.'

'Another customer?' Callie came up. The stables at the farm were full, but she always wanted more.

'It's a hard case.' The man looked sad. He looked defeated, as if he had known a lot of disappointments and could not stand any more. 'The mare is in bad trouble.'

'I'll get the Colonel,' Dora said, but Callie said, 'Let me. He hates being woken up, but at least I do it gently.'

The last time a horse was down at night and thrashing in its box, and Dora had shouted in the Colonel's ear, he had sat up and yelled, 'Messerschmitts - take cover!'

The Colonel came out of the back door with his yellow mongrel dog, pulling his worn tweed cap over sleepy eyes. He was a tall thin man with a slight limp from the war, and a scar by his eye where a kick from one of his horses had left him able to move the right side of his face more than the left, so that you could not always tell if he were serious or joking. He limped down the cinder path in his socks because he couldn't find a pair of shoes, walking on his heels with his toes turned up, because the ground was damp.

He and the bow-legged man leaned against posts with their hands in their pockets and talked quietly. Callie put a wheelbarrow in a doorway and pretended to be cleaning out Lancelot's clean stable, so that she could hear.

'. . . but I can't do any more,' the man was saying, 'because I lost my job.'

'I'm sorry.' The Colonel waited. He was a good listener.

'Down at the Pinecrest.'

The Pinecrest was an unattractive shabby hotel outside the town, with no pine trees in sight and not on the crest of a hill, but in a swampy valley where a polluted stream ran sluggishly through, gathering more pollution from the garbage that the Pinecrest cook threw out of the back door.

'I was in the stables there. They hire out riding hacks, you know.'

'Yes, I know.' The Colonel made a face as if he would rather not know.

'It's been on my mind,' the groom said. 'I done my best for my horses, but they want to get the last scrap of work out of them, and they're not fit for it.' The Colonel waited. 'Well, you can't feed more than the owner will buy, can you? The pasture is all grazed out and the hay he bought – you wouldn't use it for bedding.'

'They got a licence to run a riding stable?'

'Must do, or they couldn't be in business. I don't know how they got it though, unless they bribed the authorities, *which* I wouldn't put it past them, the kind of people they are.'

'Why did you stay with them?'

'Work's not easy to find.' The groom shrugged. 'I kept my mouth shut, because I needed the job, and my horses needed me. But then I couldn't hold myself in any longer. When I hit that boy of theirs – he was lucky I didn't kill him – they said, "Pack your bags and keep walking." '

'What happened?'

'They've got this old mare, see? A good one once. They got her off the track because she wouldn't race, and they've always kept her down and very poor, so she'd be quiet enough to ride. Quiet! The poor thing can hardly raise a canter. She gets a saddle sore, of course, with that thin thoroughbred skin and no flesh on her. Well, then it's my day off, and this fat lady comes to the hotel. "I want to ride Beauty Queen," she says. Beauty Queen, that's what they call her, though she'd win no prizes anywhere. I come back early with a bag of cracked corn I'd managed to scrounge from a friend of mine who has some poultry, and someone yells, "Hey you! Saddle up Beauty for this lady." "Her back's not healed," I says, shutting the door of my car quick, so they wouldn't see the bag of corn and grab it to make porridge for the guests. "Saddle her up, I told you!" That was their eldest son, name of Todd, very ugly customer. When I refused, he gets the saddle himself and thumps it on that poor old mare's back' – the groom winced, as if he could feel the pain of it himself – 'and leads her out. I grab the rein and start to lead her back inside, and when the boy gets in the doorway to stop me, I knock him sideways.'

'Into the manure heap, I do hope.' Callie was frankly listening now, standing in Lancelot's doorway with a foot on the barrow handle and her chin on the fork.

'Right.' The groom smiled for the first time, then turned back to the Colonel with a long face. 'So I lost my job, and the horses lost me, and Beauty – well, God knows what will happen to her.'

'What about the RSPCA?'

'The Inspector is away. I can't wait, because I'm leaving for Scotland first thing tomorrow. I've a pal up there might have a job for me. So I came to you, because I'd heard what you do here for horses. Will you help?'

'Oh Lord,' the Colonel said. 'I'll try.' He hated trouble and this looked like trouble, but for a horse, he would get into trouble with both feet. Last year, he had got himself knocked out at Westerham Fair, taking on a giant of a man who was dragging off a mare in foal tied to the tail gate of a lorry.

3

'Remember when you pulled that chap out of the driver's cab and found out how big he was?' Steve laughed, remembering, as they drove next day down the long winding hill and headed towards the Pinecrest Hotel.

The Colonel grinned with the agile side of his face. 'I wouldn't have tackled him if I'd known.'

'You would.' Steve drove fast and cheerfully. He liked to drive the little sports car, which the Colonel wasted by driving too cautiously, and he loved to go on rescue missions like this. It made his nerves hum and his body feel light and strong at the same time. If he had lived in olden days, he would have gone off hacking at dragons with a two-bladed sword.

'Don't drive so fast,' the Colonel said. 'I've got to think out how I'm going to handle this.'

'Why can't we just march in, demand to see the horses, and if the mare's condition is as bad as the groom said, take her away? I could start leading her home while you go back for the horse box.'

'And get charged with – let's see: forcing an entry,' the Colonel ticked it off on his fingers, 'breach of the peace – that's if you get into a fight – trespassing, horse stealing. No, Steve, we've got to be very careful to stay on the right side of the law.'

'Oh that.' Steve shifted impatiently. When he was younger, he had got into a lot of trouble for not caring which side was which. 'The mare is in a bad way. That's what counts.'

'We've got to do it right.' The Colonel bit at the skin

round his nails, a habit that Callie's mother Anna had been trying to get rid of since she married him. He remembered, and put the hand down into his jacket pocket. 'I've got twenty other horses and ponies to think of. No help to them if I get my stable closed down.'

'No one would do that. Everyone's proud of the farm.'

'You'd be surprised, Steve. There are people round here who'd be glad to see us go out of business. They think the farm is a waste of money and a waste of land. Unproductive. Plough it under and raise wheat for the starving millions.'

'Couldn't grow much wheat in our chalky soil.'

'Face it, Steve,' the Colonel said gloomily, biting his nails again. 'There are people who don't like horses. Incredible, but true. Horses smell. They bring flies. They give you asthma. One end kicks and the other end bites. They get through gaps in hedges and go across people's land.'

'Old Beckett.'

'If a brewery Clydesdale with feet the size of Stroller's went over *your* lettuce seedlings, you wouldn't be so keen on horses either. These people at the Pinecrest sound very tricky. I can't risk any trouble. So back me up, Steve. Try and look like the assistant to the Agricultural and Domestic Animals County Surveyor.'

'Who's he?'

'I've just invented him.'

'Good morning to you!' The Colonel was always at his most polite when he was nervous. 'Am I speaking to the lady of the house?'

The elderly woman who was crouched over a weedy flower-bed outside the hotel looked up, brushing back wild grey hair.

'If you mean Mrs H.,' she said, 'I think she's in the kitchen discussing menus with the cook. Listen – you'll hear plates and saucepan lids flying. I merely live here. But there's nothing to do and the garden is so run down, I thought I'd give myself some bending exercise, at least.'

She began to get up, clutching her back and groaning, and the Colonel gallantly helped her to her feet.

'If you've come about taking rooms—' she looked suspiciously at the Colonel and Steve.

'No, we – er, we've come to see—'

"—my advice to you is forget it.'

She paddled off in grey gym shoes with her toes turned out. The hotel door had opened, and an anxious little woman with nervous hands and a twitching mouth had come out.

'Dear Mrs Ogilvie.' She tried a laugh. 'Quite a joker. No need to take any notice of what she says. She's a bit – *you* know.' She tapped her head, which was done up in pink rollers.

'Too true.' Mrs Ogilvie spun round in the gym shoes. 'Anyone must be to stay in this dump.'

'She's been here for five years,' Mrs Hammond whispered. 'We can't get her out of the bridal suite. But come in, do. Mustn't keep you standing. It looks like rain.' She put out a hand and squinted suspiciously up at an innocently blue sky. 'Come into the office and let's see what we can do for you.'

She was all smiles and pleasantries, and so was her husband when he came into the office, summoned by a maid who opened a door and yelled down an echoing stone passage, 'Mr H! You're wanted up front!'

After what the groom had told them, Steve and the Colonel were surprised to find him quite an agreeable man, a bit soapy and smiling too much, with an oiled wave in his hair and small pointed teeth like a saw, but not the mean and brutish tyrant they had expected.

The Colonel was thrown out of gear. They chatted politely about nothing much, and although he kept trying to start his piece about the Agricultural and Domestic Animals County Surveyor, he could never quite get it out. Instead of being put at his ease by the smiling Hammonds, he was even more nervous. He shifted his feet. He blew his nose. He bit round his nails – what a giveaway. Steve wanted to slap at his hand as Anna would have done.

When Mr Hammond finally stopped vapourizing about the weather and taxes and asked him, 'And what can I do for you, sir?' the Colonel lost his nerve completely and blurted out, 'Well, it's like this. I'm from the Home of Rest for Horses, up at Follyfoot Farm.'

That did it. Steve had told him at least twice. 'Keep quiet about the farm, till we see the mare.' But Mr Hammond said without relaxing his smile, 'I know that, of course.'

'You know the Colonel?' Steve asked, surprised.

'Oh yes, I've heard a lot about the Brigadier.' Mr Hammond deliberately upgraded him. 'It's wonderful work you're doing up there.'

'Yes indeed, very wonderful. The poor dumb beasts.' Mrs Hammond's anxious eyes misted over slightly under the rollers.

'Of course,' said the Colonel, trying to get the talk round his way, 'most of my horses are past working, but in a stable like yours, they have to earn their keep.'

'You've hit it on the nail, Brigadier,' Mr Hammond complimented him as if he had said something clever. 'I'm not a rich man, but I feed the best. Hard food, hard grooming, hard work, and what do you get?'

The Colonel's eyes were glazing over. They were all sitting down, too comfortable, and Mrs Hammond had sent the noisy maid for coffee. Would they ever get out to the stables?

'What do you get? I'll tell you what you get.' Mr Hammond, with his long glossy sideburns and his smiling sharp teeth, was an unstoppable tap of horse hokum. 'You get a fit horse, as you and I, sir, very well know, eh? Eh, lad?' He winked at Steve, as if this was a chummy secret.

The Colonel cleared his throat desperately. 'How about stable help? Hard to get these days.'

'You've hit the nail again, Brigadier. I'm not a rich man, but I pay the best. But they don't want to work, that's where it is. Had to get rid of a chap just the other day. Lazy! You've no idea. And when my son had to speak to him about neglecting the horses, he went for the boy. Like a madman, Brigadier. He had to go. I'm running the stable now with my boys, though one's still at school. Too much for me, with the hotel as well, but the horses come first.'

'I'd love to see them.' The Colonel stood up quickly and moved towards the passage door, but Mr Hammond was quicker.

'Flattered, Brigadier, flattered.' He moved casually but swiftly in front of the door. 'A man of your experience, interested in our modest—'

'I am,' said the Colonel firmly. 'Let's have a look at 'em.'

Still smiling, still soapy, Mr Hammond managed to say No without saying it. 'Feeding time . . . highly sensitive animals . . . nervous when they're disturbed. . . .' The coffee arrived right on cue, and the Colonel and Steve had to sit down again and drink it. It was as soapy as its owner, with scummy milk and bitter grounds. Steve's cup had lipstick on it.

They left in a flurry of smiles and compliments. 'So kind of you to drop in . . . always nice to swap horse yarns. . . .' and a shout from the grey-haired lady who was back in the flower-bed, cutting everything down with a pair of rusty sheep shears, 'I didn't think you'd stay!'

Steve drove out by the back gate, past the stables, a patched together, rickety line of uneven sheds with a couple of thin horses in a yard outside, nosing sadly about in the trodden mud. Bales of mouldy hay were piled in an open shed. A boy was leaning against them, a cigarette smoking on his hanging lip.

It was the boy Lewis, who had tripped Callie up in the yard at the farm.

4

'He bluffed me out,' the Colonel said.

'That wasn't difficult,' Steve said glumly.

'Don't talk to the Colonel like that,' Anna said, and the Colonel said, 'He's right. I was a flop.'

They were all sitting round the kitchen table at the farmhouse, trying to work out the next move. Anna, the Colonel's wife and Callie's mother, with her long pale hair pinned on top of her head. Callie in her school uniform, trying to do homework and be part of the talk at the same time. Steve disgusted, but eating slice after slice of home-made bread as Anna cut it. Dora with her untidy hair and brown blunt face, two puppies snoring in her lap. Little Slugger Jones, ex-jockey, ex-boxer, who worked with Steve and Dora in the stables.

'He wants to keep his nose out of trouble,' Slugger said. 'That's what he wants to do.' He had been punched about so much in his boxing days that he could no longer talk directly to anybody, only to himself.

'That's no help to that poor mare,' Dora said.

'There she goes again.' Slugger munched cake with his gums. He was losing his teeth and hair at an equal rate. 'All excited over hearsay talk.'

'Slugger might be right, you know,' the Colonel said. 'Sometimes he is. How do we know that groom was telling the truth?'

'Of course he was. You heard him.' Callie drew beautiful lines under her Earth Science heading, but could write nothing more.

'Suppose he was trying to get back at them for sacking him?'

'But *suppose—*' Callie was having an idea – 'suppose those boys came up on the bike yesterday because they thought the groom might be here?'

'Good grief, she's brilliant,' Dora said.

Steve said, 'She's almost human.'

'That boy Steve saw at the Pinecrest. Lewis. Louse. I've seen him too, but I can't think where. He's no good. Oh, Colonel.' She still called him that, although he was her step-father. 'Please – you must go back!'

'When the Cruelty to Animals man gets home—'

'It can't *wait*!'

'That wretched mare—'

'An infected sore on a thoroughbred—'

They rounded on him, Dora, Steve, Callie, even Anna, who was quickly moved to pity.

'I can't get in. He'll bar the way with those teeth.'

'Pretend you want to hire a horse.'

'I can't. They know me.'

'But they don't know *me*.' Dora stood up, spilling sleepy puppies. 'I wasn't here when the boys came. "Good morning, Mr Hammond, I want to hire a hack" (anyone got any money?) "Certainly, madam." "Let me see all your horses, and I'll choose." '

'They'll rumble you,' Steve said. 'One look at your hands, and they'll know you work in a stable.'

'No they won't. I'll go disguised as one of those silly women who say they can ride and then don't even know how to hold the reins. Anna – lend me those pink flowered pants.'

'Yes, and that nylon top with the frills.'

'What on my feet?'

'Those plastic sandals Corinne left.'

'Long dangly earrings.'
'Lots of makeup.'
'Nail varnish.'
'Scent. My "Passion Flowers".
'Love beads.'
'A hair ribbon.'
'You're putting me off my tea.' Dora pushed away her plate. 'But I'll do it. For poor old Beauty Queen, I'll do it.'

Steve drove her in the farm truck to a crossroads half a mile from the Pinecrest Hotel, and got her bicycle out of the back.

'Be sure and wait for me,' she told him. 'I'm not going to ride this thing ten miles home and up that hill. Especially in this outfit.'

Dora never wore anything but jeans and sweaters and old shirts of Steve's that had shrunk in the wash. She had one skirt for going home to her mother. She felt ridiculous in the flowered pants and the earrings, with the garish eye make-up and the pale shiny lipstick and silver nail varnish with which Anna and Callie had prepared her as carefully as if she were a film star going on the set. The 'Passion Flowers' scent made her slightly sick. Horses were her natural perfume.

She approached the Pinecrest stables doubtfully, but the man who came out greeted her without surprise.

'Looking for someone, dear?'

'I want to hire a horse to go for a horseback ride,' said Dora in the kind of voice someone would have who would go riding dressed like this.

'All right, dear,' said the man, still unsurprised. First bad mark to him. If he ran a decent riding stable, he would have said, Go home and get a proper outfit.

'My friend told me you had beautiful animals here.' Girls who looked like this always had 'my friend' who told them this or that fantasy. The man was grinning as if he liked girls who looked like this, so Dora risked a seductive smile and a bit of a hip swing through the muddy yard. 'Might I see them all?'

'Come along in, my dear.'

Steve had said, 'Yuch!' when Dora got into the truck with him, but Mr Hammond ('Call me Sidney') seemed to find her divine.

The stables were what you would expect of a second-rate riding school just managing to sneak in under the law. Outside, a scrubby paddock with a trodden ring and a few flimsy jumps made of oil drums and old doors. Inside, jerry-built loose boxes with no windows, and narrow standing stalls, with a clay floor stamped into holes and hillocks. Woodwork chewed from boredom – or hunger. Scanty, dirty bedding. Flies. Thin horses with dusty coats, many of them with telltale patches of white where the hair had grown in over an old sore. As far as Dora could see, most of them needed shoeing.

'What a pretty horse. Oh, I like that spotted one. Why is he waving his head like that? What's he trying to say? Ah, the wee pony. Got the moth a bit, hasn't he?'

As Sidney Hammond showed her round the stable, she made stupid remarks to disguise what she thought. Some of the horses were fat enough, the chunky, cobby kind who wouldn't lose weight if you fed them diet pills; but many of them were ribby and hippy, gone over at the knee, and you could tell by their eyes that they had lost hope. Dora wanted to untie all their broken and knotted rope halters, let them all out, and herd them slowly back to the farm, wobbling behind them on her bicycle.

But, as the Colonel said, 'Face it, everyone isn't like us. If we took away every horse that wasn't kept by our standards, we'd have half the horses in the county up here.'

And she was here to look at Beauty Queen. That was her job.

And Sidney Hammond, although ignorant and probably miserly, was quite nice to his horses. He slapped them on their bony rumps and thin ewe necks, and told tall tales about their breeding and performance.

'This little grey. Irish bred. What a goer across country! Now here's a bay mare. Perfect lady's hack. Suit you all the way, she would. Todd!' He shouted towards the tack room, where a transistor radio was blasting.

A tall weedy boy with a feeble growth of beard appeared in the doorway. 'What do you want?' he shouted back. He inspected Dora from head to foot and back up again, and favoured her with a breathy wolf whistle.

'Get the tack for Penny.'

'Oh, just a moment, there's one horse I didn't give a sugar lump to.' In a dark corner box, Dora had spotted an unmistakable thoroughbred head beyond the cobwebby bars. She ran down the littered aisle, stumbling in the loose sandals. Before Sidney could reach her, she slid back the bolt and went into the box, where a thin chestnut mare rested a back leg in the dirty straw, wearing a torn rug.

'Why is she wearing pyjamas?' Dora looked innocently up at Sidney. Anna had put so much black stuff on her lashes that she could hardly see.

'Keep her warm, love.'

'But she's sweating. Let me—'

'Best not touch her,' Sidney said quickly. 'She's nervous.'

'Oh, I'm not afraid of her.' She reached up and quickly but carefully folded the rug back on to the neck of the mare, who jumped away in pain.

No wonder. The saddle sore on her high withers was two or three inches wide, oozing and raw.

'Oh God!' Dora said in her normal voice, but Sidney Hammond was too busy explaining to notice.

'Looks worse than it is. All my groom's fault. I sacked him for letting it get so bad. It's clearing up with this new ointment.'

'Have you had the vet?'

'Of course, love.' When he was telling a full scale lie, his mouth went on smiling, but his eyes did not.

'He can't be much good. I know someone who could help.'

'I'm not a rich man, you know. I can't afford these huge fees.'

'No, I mean at Follyfoot Farm. The place where they have the old horses.'

'But Beauty Queen isn't old.' If Mr Hammond guessed at a connection between Dora and the Colonel, his soft-soaping smile didn't show it.

'They might take her though. I know a boy—' Dora lowered the heavy lashes coyly – 'a boy who works there. Shall I ask?'

Mr Hammond sighed, and surrendered. 'If it's best for Beauty. I'm up to my neck here, short-handed, all these animals and a hotel full of guests. . . .'

He started to cover the mare's back, but Dora said, 'Let's take off the rug and put ointment on, and a clean rag or something.'

'You're a great girl.' Sidney squeezed her hand. 'A real little Samaritan.'

When they left the box, the bay mare was drooping between pillar reins, with a long-cheeked curb bridle and an ugly old saddle that made Beauty's back understandable.

'You pay in advance,' said smiling Sidney.

'How much?'

'Seventy-five pence to you, my dear.'

'Oh, I'm afraid that's too much.'

Some other people had come to ride, three women in tight jodhpurs who looked as if they were housewives hoping to lose weight, and other horses were being saddled.

Sidney lowered his voice. 'Fifty pence then, but keep it dark.'

'Oh *no*,' said Dora, glad to find a way out of riding poor Penny, although she would only have taken her round the nearest corner and let her graze for an hour. 'That wouldn't be fair on you. I'll come back when I'm not so broke. I'll ring up the farm about Beauty. Don't worry.'

She ducked under Penny's pillar rein and got herself out to the yard, where one of the housewives already had her stout thighs across a hairy cob with its eyes half shut. Dora paused briefly to let out a couple of links in its curb chain, and ran – slop, slop in the plastic sandals – to her bicycle.

'Don't forget to come back, my dear!' Sidney Hammond was in the stable doorway, smiling and waving.

5

'And perhaps I will,' Dora said. 'Don't laugh, but I quite liked him. He was nice to me.'

Beauty Queen had been brought up to the farm, Sidney Hammond profuse with thanks, blessings, promises to pay whatever he could ('though I'm not a rich man'), and make endowments in his will.

'I've got to laugh,' Steve said. 'You had him cornered and he knew it. He had to be nice.'

'He fancied me.'

'Hah!' said Steve. 'Listen to that, Callie. Get her all dressed up, and look what happens.'

'It was the Passion Flowers.' Callie was standing on a box, very tenderly smoothing the ointment the vet had prescribed on to the chestnut mare's back. 'It went to her head.'

Callie had inherited from her mother a natural gift for caring for sick or injured animals. Beauty Queen, rechristened Miss America, was in the foaling stable behind the barn, and since Steve and Dora and Slugger were busy enough, it was Callie's job to clean the wound with warm water and hydrogen peroxide, and put on ointment and antiseptic powder.

She got up earlier to take care of Miss before she went to school, and rushed straight back to the mare as soon as she got home on the bus, so that her uniform was always smeared with ointment and powder and her school shoes full of bedding.

When Anna complained, Callie said, 'Then don't make me go to school.'

She had never liked the big rough school on the outskirts of the manufacturing town which lay farther along the valley; but it was the only one, unless she went to boarding school, and Callie would not hear of leaving the farm.

This year, school was worse than ever. There was a rotten gang of older boys who were always in trouble, except with those teachers who were afraid of them, and who got themselves through the boredom of the day by terrorizing some of the younger children. The sneaky kids sneaked, and got beaten up. The fighting kids fought back, and got left alone. The others simply tried to keep clear of the bullies. Callie was one of the others.

But one day when she was sitting on the playground wall reading, because she got all the exercise she needed at the farm, and she hated games with balls because she was short-sighted, a foot suddenly came up underneath the open book and sent it flying.

Three big brutish boys scrummed for it, knocking each other down, and when they got up, howling like inane hyenas, the book and cover were in shreds.

It was a library book and she would have to pay for it, but Callie walked away in silence, stretching her eyes to keep tears back.

'Hey!' A hand took her arm and spun her round. 'I know you, stupid cry-baby!'

'Let me go. I'll scream.'

'Try it.' The boy guffawed. 'We'll give you something to scream about.' He had a broad stupid face, with a pudgy nose and thick hanging lips. It was Lewis the Louse. This was where she had seen him before. Hanging about with the bad crowd. This school was so big that you couldn't know all the names, nor even all the faces.

'Yeah.' He dropped her arm, staring. 'I do know you. You live up the hill, doncher?'

Callie nodded, sick with fear. The three large boys stood round her. With such a shrieking mob in the playground, no one would see or hear whatever they did to her.

'You belong to that chap with the gimpy leg – haw haw, jolly good show and all that sort of rot.' The Louse did a rotten imitation of what he thought would be the voice of someone like the Colonel.

'My mother is married to him.'

'Oh girls! It's too romantic.' Lewis snuffled in his horrible blocked-up nose. Then he leaned forward and put his face so close to Callie's that she could see all the pimples and open pores. 'You know who I am, doncher?'

She nodded, staring at him like a rabbit.

'Your lot tried to make trouble for us. Remember that, you guys.' He jerked his head at his friends, who were even uglier and stupider (if possible) than him. 'We don't like this person.'

'But I'm taking care of your horse!' Callie was bolder, thinking of poor Miss America, who was her life's purpose at the moment.

'Quite right,' said Lewis, 'quite right. And we'll take care of you. Don't forget it.'

He snapped his thick grubby finger in Callie's face and sauntered off, his friends behind him, singing a crude song, whose key words they changed briefly while they passed a teacher, and then took up again.

When Callie was really upset, she couldn't talk about it. All she could do was to say she had a bad headache the next day, and all this got her was that Anna made her stay in bed and would not let her go out to the stable to take care of Miss America.

She knew that Callie had not got a headache. That was why she did that. And because she knew she hadn't got a headache, she sat on Callie's bed in the dark that night and asked her what was wrong.

'Oh – nothing. It's just school.' Callie tossed about, and the kitten who was on the bottom of the bed made a pounce at her toes.

'Was there trouble? Work, or what?'

Usually Callie did not like to have her hair touched, but when her mother stroked it at night, it was all right.

She shook her head under the stroking hand. How was it you could manage not to cry until someone gave you sympathy? It ought to be lack of sympathy that made you cry.

'What then?'

Callie sniffed. 'It's just – oh, I hate the kids.'

'Aren't there any friends?'

'I'm not the type that makes friends, you know that. All my friends are here. Most of them have got four legs.'

'You ought to have friends your own age.' All mothers worry once in a while that their child is 'different', though they wouldn't really like it if they weren't. 'Perhaps we should think about boarding school.'

'Mother, you promised.'

'Let's see how things go then.'

6

But things did not go any better. They went worse. Wherever Callie went, Lewis and his gang seemed to be there, jeering at her, tripping her up, jumping out from behind lockers, tweaking a pigtail as they ran by.

One day she was changing classrooms, going upstairs as Lewis was coming down, and he bumped into her so hard that he knocked her back down the stairs. She caught the rail and steadied herself against the wall. The rest of her class went on up the stairs. In this school, if you saw trouble brewing, you got out of the way.

'What do you want?' Callie stood against the wall with her hands spread out as if she was going to be shot. When she was afraid, it went to her stomach. She thought she was going to bring up her lunch all over the Louse's elastic-sided boots.

'Don't be afraid, little girl.' He put on a kind of leer which he thought was a smile. 'I got a present for you.'

Callie managed to say, 'Oh?' and swallowed her lunch back down.

'Knowing how much you love our four-footed friends—' from behind his back he held out a parcel wrapped in newspaper – 'I brought this for you.'

Callie took it, watching him.

'Go on. Open it. You'll like it, really.'

It smelled peculiar, but Callie gingerly unwrapped the newspaper and saw that she was holding the hoof of a dead horse. Where it had been cut off, it was congealed with black blood and dirt.

She wrapped it up again quickly and handed it back to Lewis. She could not speak.

'Don't you recognize it?' he jeered. 'You should do. I thought you was so fond of poor old Beauty Queen.'

'You couldn't—' she whispered.

'It's still our horse, ain't it? Too bad you didn't take better care of her, for we had to have her destroyed this morning. Very 'umane. A merciful release.' He shoved the newspaper bundle back into Callie's hands and ran away.

She could not believe him. Yet she had to believe him. It was a narrow, well-bred hoof, the pale colour that goes with a chestnut's white leg. She must telephone her mother. Yet she could not telephone her mother. As long as she didn't hear the truth, it still could be not true.

After she had been sick in the cloakroom, she went down to the basement furnace and got a shovel, and buried the hoof in the newspaper under the bushes behind the goal posts. Then she went back to her classroom.

'Where on earth—' Miss Golding began, then saw Callie's face.

'I was sick.'

Immediately there was a clamour from the class of, 'I knew that sausage was off', 'It was the spuds, they boil 'em in the dish-water', 'You won't catch me eating their treacle roll.'

'Do you want to lie down? Shall I ring up your home?'

'I'm all right.' Callie sat down.

At the end of the day, she went to the bus like a sleep-walker, and sat at the back, staring straight ahead, not looking out of the window all the way to ride a cross-country course alongside the road, as she usually did. The bus climbed the hill and stopped by the gate of the farm.

'Give my love to the old horses,' the driver said, as he always did.

'Thank you,' Callie said, as she always did. She went under the stone arch and walked across the yard going towards the house. Her mother would be starting supper. She would turn from the stove and Callie would know at once from her face whether it was true.

Several horses called to her. Cobbler's Dream in the corner box banged on his door and swung his head with the flashy white blaze up and down to get her attention. She was almost to the corner of the yard where the path came in from the house when Steve backed out of the Weaver's stable, dragging a loaded barrow.

'Hi!' he shouted. 'Aren't you going to see your patient?'

Callie turned slowly round.

'Her back looks much better today. You're doing a good job.'

Callie ran. It was not until she was in the loose box with her head against Miss America's thin thoroughbred neck that she began to cry.

After the Easter holidays started, Callie told her mother that she could not stay at that school.

'I'd better start finding out about boarding schools.'

'We can't afford it.'

'No.' Anna laughed. 'But you could try for a scholarship.'

'I'm not clever enough.'

'We'll see.'

They did not discuss it any more. Why spoil the holidays? The days were roofed with blue sky and whipped cream clouds. The old horses luxuriated in the sun on their dozing backs. Callie rode Cobbler's Dream, and the mule, and Hero the circus horse, and anyone else who was rideable, and she and Steve and Dora jogged up to the higher hills where the turf was patched with rings of white and yellow flowers, like fried eggs.

Miss America's back was healed and they could ride her too. Fleshed out and well fed, she was a pleasant ride, although her thoroughbred stride had been stiffened by pounding on roads, and from the way she chucked up her head, you could guess at the kind of hands that had tugged at her reins.

They rode her in a snaffle, bareback to make sure of not hurting her, and the mare flourished in the warm spring.

'But there's always a fly in the ointment,' Dora said.

The fly was Sidney Hammond, arriving with a lopsided trailer with the tailboard tied with rope, to take back his mare.

'Don't let her go.' Steve and Dora cornered the Colonel in the tack room when he went to get a halter.

'It's his horse. We've done what we set out to do. He's very busy, he says. He's getting a lot of people from town, secretaries and things wanting to go pony trekking at weekends. He needs the mare.'

'She isn't a pony.'

'Dora. Don't *try* to annoy me.' The Colonel did not want Miss America to go either.

Mr Hammond was as smiley and ingratiating as ever, as well he might be, since he hadn't paid a penny for the mare's keep, in spite of all his blessings and promises.

Dora kept out of his sight, in case she might need to put on the pink pants and 'Passion Flowers' disguise again to go and check on Miss America when she was back at the Pinecrest as Beauty Queen. Steve helped Mr Hammond load the mare, making a big fuss about spreading straw on the rotting tailboard in case of splinters.

As the trailer pulled away, he said, 'What a hunk of junk,' loud enough for Mr Hammond to hear, but smiling Sidney merely waved and grinned, and leaned out of the car window to call once again, 'I can never thank you enough, Brigadier!'

'I'll send you a bill!' the Colonel called after him, not loud enough to hear.

'You know he won't,' Slugger grumbled, sweeping up the old manure that Steve had kicked out of the van before he would lead Miss America in. 'You know he's too soft with these folk who could well pay to help out them as can't.'

'Shut up, Slugger,' the Colonel said. 'You know we only ask people to pay what they can afford.'

'And that one could well afford.'

'I said I'd send him a bill.'

'Oh yes, just like he sent in a bill to that old clothes and firewood chap as brought the pony in here for two weeks rest and we had the beggar all winter. Have us all in Queer Street, that lot will. Oh yes, he says. Send in a bill, he says. . . .' Slugger grumbled away, sweeping the gravel before him with short testy jabs.

7

It was Dora's birthday. She had wanted to spend it at the farm, but her mother wanted her at home, so she had to put on her skirt and go down into the town.

Her mother, who was still hoping that she would grow out of horses, although there was no evidence, at seventeen, that she ever would, had assembled a group of 'interesting' people to try to show her the kind of life she was missing.

A girl from an art school, starved and pale, with round glasses like wheel rims and a long dusty dress with a trodden hem. Two serious boys with bushy beards who were teaching problem children to get rid of their problems by screaming and hitting each other. A few grown-ups whose mouths kept on opening and shutting long after Dora had stopped listening.

She was so bored that she ate too much to pass the time, fell asleep on the bus going home, and was carried past the village where she was supposed to change buses.

'Where are we?' She woke with a start as the driver braked round a sharp corner.

He stopped at the next cross-roads and showed her a lane which led to the main road, where she might get another bus back.

It was late afternoon, with twilight settling on the budding hedges in the valley, and damp beginning to rise from the ground through the new spring grass. Dora walked by the side of the road, getting her feet wet. She was not sure where she was, but when she went over a bridge, she thought she might be crossing the sluggish brown river that ran by the

Pinecrest Hotel. If there were no buses on the main road, she would get a lift from the first car that would stop.

'Come back with her throat cut one day, she will,' Slugger Jones always grumbled when Dora turned up from town in a strange car or on the back of a motor-bike.

'There are some weird people about these days,' Anna warned, but Dora said, 'No weirder than me,' and went on hitch-hiking.

She had promised to be back for supper. After that lunch, she could never eat again. But Anna had made a cake. And there would be no 'interesting' people with 'stimulating' talk. Just people who knew each other well, and were sure of being liked.

Behind her in the lane, she heard the clop-clop of a trotting horse, that always stirring sound that brings people to their windows or out to the gate, even if they have their own horses to clop-clop with.

Dora turned and stood still to watch it come by. As the man and horse came into view out of the dusk, she saw that it was Miss America. Dora stepped out into the road and held up her hand like a school crossing patrol man.

The mare stopped of her own accord. She was not so much being ridden, as carrying an unsteady rider, who nearly pitched over her head when she stopped.

'Whoops.' He clung round Miss America's neck and smiled foolishly at Dora, who saw that he was drunk. She also saw that the saddle with which he had so little contact was a heavy broken thing, well down on the mare's bony withers.

Dora saw red. She grabbed the man's arm and pulled him off the horse. He was half-way off anyway.

'Thanks.' He landed on his feet, with the luck of a drunk. 'I was wondering whether to get on the ground or back in the saddle.'

'You shouldn't be *in* that saddle.' Furiously, Dora

unbuckled the girth and lifted off the saddle. The sore back had broken open again, raw and bleeding.

Dora swore. 'Here – just a minute—' The man lurched at her, but she went to the side of the road and pitched the dreadful old saddle over a thick hedge into the bushes.

'Now look what you've done!' The man's red face was woeful. 'How am I going to ride this thing home?'

'You're not,' Dora said.

'Have to walk then.' Strengthening himself with a swig from a flask in his breeches pocket, he looped the reins over his arm and started off down the road. The mare was slightly lame.

Dora followed a short distance behind. The man weaved down the lane in the failing light, staggering now and then and propping himself up with a hand on the mare's neck. When he came to the main road, he stood for a while watching the cars go past, turning his head from side to side as if he were at a tennis match.

Dora watched him. Finally he seemed to make up his mind. He took the reins over Miss America's head and tied them very carefully round a signpost. Then he stepped into the road with his arm raised, outlined unsteadily in the lights of a car. The luck of a drunk still held. The car stopped, and he got in and was driven away.

Dora untied the mare and they walked along the grass at the side of the road until they came to the Dog & Whistle, where Dora could telephone for Steve to bring the horse box.

In the farmhouse, Callie greeted her. 'I got you a present. Want to see?'

'Thanks. I got you one too. Want to see?'

'Where?'

'In the foaling stable.'

'A new customer!' Callie ran out.

Dora asked Anna, 'Is – er, is the Colonel in a good mood?'

'He was,' Anna said. 'What have you brought home?'

'Miss America,' Dora said. 'Her back has broken down again.'

The Colonel did not say much. He waited to see what would happen. When nothing happened, he telephoned the Pinecrest Hotel.

'Good morning, Brigadier. Nice to hear your voice.'

'I've got your mare.'

'That's good of you.'

'Her back is almost as bad as it was before.'

'That fellow – that stupid drunk – it's all his fault. I tell you, Brigadier, this riding school game is one long headache.'

'What happened?'

'I wish I knew. He came back here with a hangover and a cockeyed story about losing the saddle and tying the horse to a signpost. He'd been back to all the signposts on all the side turnings along the main road, and when the mare wasn't there and wasn't here in the stable, he thought he'd imagined the whole thing, and swore to go on the wagon.'

'Good.' The Colonel waited.

Mr Hammond waited too. Finally he said, 'I thought the mare might have run to you, seeing she was so well kept there before. I'm grateful, Brigadier.'

'You want me to keep her?'

'You know I'm short-handed here.'

'So am I.'

'But your staff is reliable. I work my fingers to the bone, but I have to leave a lot to my boys, and – well, you know what they are these days. You can't trust them with anything. Especially a valuable horse like Beauty.' He would not even stick up for his own family. 'So if you could do me a favour, Brigadier, I'll pay anything you want.'

'You didn't pay the last bill,' the Colonel murmured without moving his lips. He hated talking about money.

'The cheque is in the post.'

Mr Hammond rang off cheerfully, with best wishes to all for the Easter season. The man was incredible. He had no shame at all.

'He's not going to get the mare back though,' the Colonel said. 'But somehow I don't think he'll ask.'

'I worry about his other horses.' Dora frowned. 'I don't see how he ever got a stable licence.'

'Perhaps he didn't,' Steve said. 'Why don't you ask the County Council, Colonel?'

'They'll think I'm suspicious.'

'Well, you are.'

At the County Council, they told him that the Pinecrest's application for a riding-stable licence was on the files, awaiting an inspection.

'Our regular man is off sick. I wonder, Colonel – I know you're a busy man, but you're fully qualified, and I'm sure the hotel wants to get it cleared up before the summer.'

So the Colonel and Steve went back to the Pinecrest Hotel. He refused to take Dora in the sandals and earrings, but he did take Steve in case of trouble.

There was no trouble. He had written authority to inspect the stable. He spent half a day there, with Sidney Hammond following him affably round and thanking him at the end for his time and trouble with a smile like the jaws of a gin trap.

The Colonel turned in an honest and detailed report. It was not his decision whether or not to grant the licence.

8

Since last year, when Cobbler's Dream had captured a thief and saved his own life by clearing the impossible spiked park fence, Steve had begun to jump him again.

The Cobbler had once been a famous juvenile show jumper. When the girl who trained him grew too big, he was bought by a hard-handed child who wanted a vehicle for winning championships, rather than a pony to love. Steve worked for her father. He had to see the marvellous pony making mistakes because of the child. Finally he had to see him blinded in one eye by a blow from a whip. He had taken him away then, and brought him to the farm, and they had both stayed here.

The other eye became half blind, but Cobby had adapted so well that he was almost as surefooted as before, and his fantastic leap over the Manor park fence had proved that he had acquired some kind of sixth sense to judge a jump. He would jump almost anything if you took him slow and let him get the feel of it.

Steve put up some sheep hurdles in one of the fields, and he and Dora made a brush jump with gorse stuck through a ladder. Most of the other horses were too old and stiff to jump, so Dora was teaching the mule Willy, who had no mouth at all, and either rushed his jumps flat out or stopped dead and let Dora jump without him.

Steve and Dora had the afternoon off, so they took the Cobbler and Willy through the woods on the other side of their hill, where there were fallen tree trunks across the rides.

Cobby jumped them all without checking his canter, bunching his muscles, arching his back, smoothly away on his landing stride with his ears pricked for the next jump. Willy jumped the smaller trees. If they did not reach right across the path, he whipped round them with his mouth open, yawing at the bit. If they were too big, he dug in his toes, and Dora had to get off and lead him over. He would jump his front end, stand and stare with the tree trunk under his middle, and then heave his rear end over with a grunt like an old man getting out of the bath.

Near the far edge of the wood, Cobby shortened his stride, trotting with his head high, and turned to the side, listening.

'What does he hear?'

There were people who came to the woods with guns and shot at rabbits and foxes and anything that moved. Sometimes they shot each other.

Steve and Dora both stopped and listened. Only the continual sigh of the breeze moving through the tops of the tall trees.

'I don't hear anything.'

'Cobb does. His hearing is sharper now that he can't see much. So is his nose.'

The chestnut pony had his nostrils squared, as if he were getting a message.

Steve pushed him on, over two more jumps, but he slowed down again, listening.

'There is something. Let's go the way he wants to.'

They rode out of the wood and along the edge of a cornfield. In a grassy lane beyond the hedge, a grey horse was grazing in a patch of clover.

It was a calm horse. It stood still and exchanged blown breaths with Cobby, and then the ritual squeal and striking out. The mule laid back his long ears like a rabbit and said nothing. He distrusted strange horses. When he was turned out with a new one, he would communicate for the first two weeks only with his heels.

The grey horse wore a head collar. It let Steve slip his belt through the noseband, and trotted quietly beside Cobby back to the farm.

The Colonel did not recognize the horse. 'Someone will be worried though,' he said. 'It's a nice-looking horse and well kept.' The grey looked like a hunter, coat clean and silky, whiskers and heels neatly trimmed, tail and mane properly pulled. 'Better ring the police, Steve.'

Sergeant Oddie said at once, 'Oh no! Not that grey again. Look here, I've got the big wedding to worry about, two men off on a drug raid, a three-car crash on the Marston road and some nippers have set fire to the bus shelter. That horse is the last thing I need.'

'It's been out before?'

'Time and again. The neighbours are on my neck about it day and night. Regular wasps' nest, it's stirred up. Here, I'll give you Mrs Jordan's number, and I wish you'd tell her how to build a fence to keep a horse in.'

'But we have,' Mrs Jordan said. 'It's not our fault, or the horse's. Oh dear. I'll come and get him.'

'I'll ride him home, if you could bring me back,' Steve said.

The grey horse looked like a lovely ride, and he was, well schooled, a beautiful mover, quickly responsive, but you could stop him by flexing your wrist.

Steve was surprised when he saw where he came from. The Jordans' house on the edge of a small town had obviously once stood in fields, but new houses had been built close all round, and the fenced paddock was not much bigger than a tennis court. The fence was strong and high enough. The gate looked sound.

'It's they who are doing it,' Mrs Jordan told Steve. 'They used to do it at night, but they're getting bolder now, and they've begun to do it in the daytime if I go out.'

'Who do what?'

'The neighbours. The people in that pink house with gnomes in the garden and plastic flowers in the window-boxes. They open the gate and let David out, then they quickly ring the Police and complain that the horse is loose and trampling on people's gardens.'

'How do you know?'

'Oh, I know all right.' Mrs Jordan was a faded, once beautiful woman, with lines of work and worry round her big sad eyes and her full, drooping mouth. 'When the police were here last time – they were nice enough at first, but now they're getting fed up – I saw that front curtain move, and another time, the woman was standing in the window, blatantly watching and laughing.'

'Why don't you padlock the gate?'

'We have. But she somehow pried the rails loose at night, and then got them back up after she'd chased David out. It's her, not her husband. He's not so bad, but she's a fanatic. She hates horses, because she thinks they're something that rich people have. Rich! She's much better off than us. Her husband is a plumber. But she's the kind of person who can't stand anybody having something she hasn't got, even if she doesn't want it. She wants to buy that piece of land where David's paddock is, and breed chinchillas.

'Chinchillas!' She looked at Steve with her tragic eyes. 'On what was once our back lawn, where the girls used to have their summer house and swings.'

After they had put the grey horse away in the open shed in the corner of the paddock, Mrs Jordan made Steve go into the house for something to eat before she would drive him home. She seemed lonely, glad of someone to talk to. He sat in a comfortable shabby armchair and listened. He had learned from the Colonel that if you will only shut up and listen, people will tell you things they won't tell to someone who is trying to keep up their end of the conversation.

It was a tragic story. Her husband had been a trainer and show judge. A car crash had killed their younger daughter and left him unable to work for a long time. They had to borrow money on their house and land. Their other daughter Nancy left college and went to work, and Mrs Jordan got a job in an old people's nursing home, but they could not pay the interest on the mortgage. Four acres of their land had been seized, and sold to the builder who had put up all these ugly little houses where the pastures and stables had been.

All the horses had gone, of course, except David, who had belonged to the dead girl.

'How could we part with him? Nancy rides him occasionally, but she has so little time, and she's always so tired. We're all tired, Steve. My husband has a part-time job now, but it doesn't pay much, and he's not well enough even for that. I lie awake night after night wondering what will happen when they take our house in the end and that horrible woman gets David's paddock – our last bit of land – and keeps her wretched chinchillas in prison cages.'

'Death row.' Steve nodded. 'Only one way out.'

'I hate her.'

'So do I,' Steve said with feeling, although he had never seen the woman with the plaster gnomes in her garden.

'Sergeant Oddie rang me up after he talked to you, and said if the horse got out again, we'd have to get rid of him.'

'I thought the sergeant was so busy,' Steve said.

'Not too busy to tell me *that*. And that's what that woman wants.'

'Why don't you turn her in?'

'I can't prove it. She's cunning. I've never been able to catch her.'

'Mind if I try?'

'It's not much use.'

'You all go out some night. Make a big noise about driving off in the car, so she knows. But I'll be here. I'll be in the shed with David.'

No need to tell the Colonel. Not that he would mind, but . . . no need to worry him.

'I can't risk any trouble,' he had said. He had his own problems with neighbours. 'We've got to stay on the right side of the law.'

Well, this was the right side, but . . . no need to tell him.

Steve did not tell Dora either, or anyone at the farm.

9

The next evening, after the horses had been bedded down and fed and watered, Steve asked if he could use the truck.

'All right,' the Colonel said. 'What for?'

'I'm going out.'

'Who with?' Dora's rumpled head came over the top of a stable door, where she was rubbing liniment on Dolly's chronic foreleg.

'A girl I know.'

'You don't know any girls.'

'How do you know?'

'You'd tell me.'

Dora rested her chin on the door. Old Doll put her head out beside her and laid back her ears at Steve. She had once been so badly abused by a man that she still only liked women. It was Dolly who had kicked the Colonel in the head.

'You'd be the last person I'd tell.' Steve laughed. 'You'd want to come too, and sit between us and talk all through the film.'

'Are you going to a film?'

'Yes.'

'I want to come too.'

'No.'

'What's her name?'

'Nancy.'

'I don't believe you're going out with a girl,' Dora said, but more doubtfully.

When he drove off, Dora was sitting on the wall by the gate, polishing a snaffle bit and kicking her heels against the bricks. Her face looked closed and sulky, her lower lip stuck out. Steve waved. She did not wave back or look up.

Mr Jordan was a grey, stooped man, with a mouth stiffened by pain of body and heart. Nancy was a bright-cheeked girl with thick bouncing hair and good legs, the kind of girl Steve would have gone to the cinema with if he had been going to the cinema with a girl.

They made the necessary noise about leaving. Racing the engine, slamming the doors, going back for a coat, calling out that they would be late.

'The film starts at eight!' Mrs Jordan called from behind the wheel, to let her neighbours know that they would be away at least two hours.

In the pink house with the window-boxes full of impossible flowers that never bloomed in the spring, nor even in England at all, a shadow moved behind the curtain.

Steve sat in the straw of the open shed and talked to the grey horse and thought about things long gone. Other nights of adventure when you waited, with your nerves on edge and your hair pricking on your scalp. The night when he had stolen Cobby away to safety with sacking wrapped round his hooves.

About nine-thirty, with the family still in the cinema, David raised his head from his hay and swung his small ears forward. Steve listened, holding his breath.

Were there footsteps on the soft ground? Did the night breeze shiver that bush, or was someone behind it? Steve watched, motionless in the dark corner.

David, who liked people, walked out of the shed in a rustle of straw and into the paddock. A thick woman in tight pants was climbing through the fence. She held out her hand as the horse went up to her and gave him something. In the still night, Steve heard his teeth on the sugar. He followed the woman as she moved quickly across the small paddock to the gate.

Steve waited. It was too dark to see much. She had her back to him, but he heard the clink of the chain on the gate. He got up quickly, went silently up behind her and said in her ear, 'Can I help you?'

'Oh my God!' The woman jumped round with a hand on the ample shelf over her heart. As she moved, Steve was almost sure that he saw her fist clench over a piece of metal that could be a key.

'What do you want?' She was breathing fast, and he could see behind her dark fringe tomorrow's imagined headlines chasing each other through her head.

WOMAN FOUND STRANGLED. HOUSEWIFE KILLED IN NEIGHBOUR'S GARDEN. SUBURBAN SLAYING, MYSTERY GROWS.

'What you – what are you doing here?' The woman must be bold to have done as much as she had, but her mouth was twitching now with nerves, because Steve was looming over her threateningly.

'I'm a friend of the family,' he said. 'The horse looked as if he might be headed for colic, so I was watching he didn't lie down. Someone might have slipped him something. People round here have been making trouble, you wouldn't believe it.'

'Oh, I know.' The woman relaxed. 'The poor Jordans, it's dreadful for them, on top of all their bad luck. I try to keep an eye on things for them, when they're not here. That's why I came out, to check on the gate fastening.'

'Oh, I see,' said Steve. 'To check the gate.'

'That's right.' The woman started to move towards her house. 'To check the gate.'

'You keep an eye on things. That's nice.'

'Well,' she said, 'one does what one can. We were all put in this world to help each other, that's what I say.'

'Oh so do I.' With a hand on the neck of the grey horse, Steve watched the woman climb through the paddock fence and go back into her own house, waggling her bottom righteously, like a good neighbour who has done her duty.

'So that's what you ought to do,' Steve told the Jordans.

They looked at each other. 'I'm no hand with electricity.' The father looked baffled.

'I'll do it.'

'She'll see you.' Mrs Jordan glanced towards the pink house. 'She sees everything.'

'I'll do it after dark. There's no moon. She won't try anything on tomorrow after the scare she got tonight. If I use a rubber hammer, I can get the insulators on without making any noise, and I'll put the battery behind the shed so she won't hear it ticking.'

Next day, Steve offered to do Anna's shopping, and bought the battery and thin wire and the insulators while he was in town.

In the evening, when he asked casually for the truck, Dora did not ask him where he was going. She had not allowed herself to ask him about the film last night, which was a good thing because he had forgotten to find out what was on.

At the Jordans he rigged up two strands of electric wire close to the paddock rails where it could not be seen. Then he turned on the battery and waited at the side of the shed.

He chirruped softly. The horse came up to the rail, put out his nose, then jumped back and snorted.

'Sorry, David.' The grey horse stood in the middle of the paddock, looking very offended. 'I had to test it.'

Two nights Steve waited in the straw, with the battery ticking softly on the other side of the shed. He dozed and woke and dozed, but he was sleepy in the daytime, and Dora made embittered remarks about people who stayed out so late with girls that they couldn't do their jobs properly.

Why not tell her and let her watch with him in the shed and share the adventure? Because she kept saying things like, 'When are we going to see this famous Nancy? Not that I care. Or is she too hideous to bring here?' Talking herself out of the adventure.

'She's gorgeous, as a matter of fact,' Steve said, irritated. 'Marvellous legs.' He winked at Slugger.

'Can't go far wrong with that.' Slugger winked at the horse he was grooming. ' "When judgin' a woman *or* a horse, you gotta look at the legs, of course." That's what me grandad used to say.'

'Anyone can have good legs.' Dora's, which were rather muscular and boyish, were covered in torn faded blue jeans, which she refused to let Anna patch, or hem at the bottom.

On the third night, Steve went to bed early – 'What's the matter? She sick of you already?' – and got up again at midnight after everyone was asleep. He stopped the truck before he got to the Jordans', and walked quietly through what was left of their garden and round the side of the house to the shed.

When he whispered, to show the horse he was there, a voice answered him.

'Nancy?'

'I couldn't sleep.' She was lying covered with straw, only her face and hair showing.

'I wanted to do this alone.' Steve came in and sat beside her.

'Why?'

'It was my idea.'

'It's my horse.'

They lay side by side in the straw and talked softly. Nancy told him about the man at work she thought she was in love with. Girls always started to tell you about other men just when you were getting interested.

Steve wriggled his fingers through the straw to find her hand.

'But he's almost old enough to be my father,' Nancy said.

Steve took her hand, and at that moment there was a blood-curdling scream from the other side of the paddock.

David jumped. Steve and Nancy scrambled up. The plump woman in the tight pants was sitting on the ground with her arms wrapped round herself like a straitjacket, rocking backwards and forwards and moaning.

'It can't have been that bad.' Steve and Nancy slid carefully under the fence and went across to her.

'Oh, I'm killed,' the woman moaned. 'Oh, my heart—'

'Just going to check up on the gate, eh?'

She looked up at Steve, her hair, disordered from bed, standing wildly up as if the electricity had gone right through it.

'Yes,' she croaked. 'One does what one can. But there are some people—' she glowered up at Nancy, still rocking and holding herself as if she might fall apart – 'some people who don't know the meaning of the word gratitude.'

After this, Steve did take Nancy to the farm at the weekend, to show her the horses.

The Colonel was delighted with her. He conducted her round himself, hands behind his back, cap over his eyes, very military. Callie was pleased with her because she asked the right questions and said, 'How lucky for Miss to have Callie to look after her,' when they visited Miss America, queening it in the orchard so that the other horses would not disturb the healing wound.

Dora was rather gruff. She took a long look at Nancy's legs, then went off to greet a family of visitors and became very busy giving them a conducted tour of all the horses.

The family, who had only come to see the donkey which had once belonged to their Uncle Fred, kept saying, 'Well, better be getting along,' but Dora dragged them on from horse to horse, so as not to have to talk to Nancy.

Soon after this, Steve got a letter from Mrs Jordan. Their telephone had been cut off because they couldn't pay the bill.

The plump woman and the plumber had put the pink house up for sale and gone away. Two days later – *'If she'd only waited two days, she could have had her revenge in chinchillas'* – Mr Jordan was asked by a friend in Australia to go out and join him on the ranch where he was breeding horses.

'*So we're all going, Steve. A new life. Free passage out if we stay two years, and they can have this poor house and make it into a pub or a Bingo hall or whatever they want. No regrets. Except about David. We sail next week. Please find him a good home and use the sale money for the farm. The best home only. I trust you.*'

David could stay out at night, so the Colonel let Steve bring him to the farm.

'What's *that*?' Dora made a face at the grey as he backed neatly out of the horse box and stood with his fine head up and his mane and tail blowing like an Arab, staring at some of the old horses, who were drawn up in the field, all pointing the same way like sheep, observing him.

'It's the horse we found on the other side of the wood. You know.'

'Nancy's horse.'

'Yes,' Steve said. 'They're—'

'It's too long in the back,' Dora said, 'and I don't like the look of that near hock.'

'They're going to Australia. With Nancy.'

'But other than that, it's the best-looking horse we've ever had here.' Dora grinned. 'Can we ride him?'

'Till we can find the right home.'

'Let's not start looking yet.'

'We've got to work with him a bit,' they told the Colonel. 'He hasn't worked for so long, we'll have to school him before we can show him to anyone.'

And every day when the Colonel, during his morning rounds, asked, 'You got a prospect for that grey?', they said, 'He's still a bit tricky. We want him perfect.'

David already was perfect. They had never had such a marvellous horse to ride. They were not going to let him go in a hurry.

'Got to work with him a bit longer.'

10

Callie had dreaded going back to school, but when the summer term started, Lewis seemed to have been converted by the glories of Easter, because he left Callie alone and did not bully her.

She watched him from a distance. He was strangely quiet. He did not make a dead set for the new, younger ones, as he usually did, twisting their arms to see if they would cry, knocking into them in the cafeteria to make them drop their food.

'School isn't so bad,' Callie told Anna. 'Perhaps I will stay.'

'Take the scholarship exam anyway.' Anna was used to Callie's frequent changes of mind. Tomorrow school might be no good again.

But tomorrow, Callie actually had a conversation with Lewis the Louse.

They were in the library, where you were not supposed to talk, but they were behind a stack of shelves and Mrs Dooley was busy at the far desk.

Lewis had taken down a book and opened it, but he did not seem able to read. Callie was searching for something in an index. She was aware that Lewis was watching her, so she looked up and smiled nervously.

To her amazement, he smiled back, his lower lip hanging on his face like a hammock, his teeth as pointed as his father's, but with gaps from fighting.

'What you do in the holidays then?' he asked.

Callie was so surprised and flummoxed that she could not think of anything.

'Oh – nothing much. I rode. I worked most of the time in the stables. I helped Steve build a gate.'

'Who's Steve?'

'The boy who works at the farm.'

'*Oh*, yeah.' Lewis nodded, remembering.

'He did a marvellous thing.' Callie babbled on, making the most of the chance to get on the right side of the Louse. 'He foiled a woman.'

'Foiled?' Lewis's mouth hung. His vocabulary was not very large.

Callie told him about the woman letting out David and then ringing the police. He listened, his slow dull eyes following the movement of her face, breathing through his mouth like a patient under anaesthetic.

'Who's talking there?' Mrs Dooley came round the end of the bookshelves. Lewis had disappeared. There was only Callie there to take a discipline mark.

Two nights later, the door of the Mongolian horse's loose box was open, and Trotsky wandered across a field of young wheat, eating it as he went and occasionally lying down for a crushing roll.

'Good thing he didn't have shoes on,' the Colonel said nervously to the farmer.

'Good thing I wasn't out there with a gun,' the farmer said grimly.

Trotsky was wily enough to undo a latch if the bolts were not fastened.

'But I know I bolted Trot's door,' Dora said. 'And the bottom bolt too, because he bit me while I was bending down.'

'Someone opened it then,' Steve said. 'Like the Jordans' neighbour.'

Callie kept her mouth shut, which was how she should have kept it behind the library shelves. Was it possible that she had put this idea for new trouble into the Louse's thick head?

He left her alone. She told her mother that she was definitely not going to take the exam. But when Lewis saw she was off her guard, he invited her one day to go with him and buy a chocolate cornet before it was time for her bus.

She went. They never got to the ice-cream van. As soon as they were round the corner from the school, Lewis pulled her into the overgrown garden of an empty house and knocked her backwards into the bushes. She picked herself up and was going to run away, but he grabbed her.

'That's just the beginning.' He stared at her with his horrid revolting slab of face.

'What for?'

'Stopping us getting a licence.'

'What do you mean?'

'Your stepfather. The Sergeant, the Bosun, whatever his daft name is. He done it.'

'It was nothing to do with the Colonel. He only sent the County Council a report on your stable.'

'He wouldn't know one end of a stable from the other.' Lewis was gripping her arm so hard that she would scream if it went on. 'Much less a horse.'

'Let me go!'

'He's got it in for us. Trying to keep an honest man from earning a crust of bread, my Dad says. We've lost a lot of bookings, you know.' His gorilla brow came down threateningly. 'People come to us for the riding.'

'Why don't you clean the place up and apply for another licence?' Callie bit her lip. Her arm was going numb. She would not scream.

'There's nothing wrong with our place,' Lewis growled.

'It's your stepfather, that's who there's something wrong with. We'd ought to put him out of business too. Perhaps we will. Yeah.' He dropped her arm, frowning under the weight of what passed for thoughts. 'Perhaps we will. My Dad says it's a crime to keep them poor old horses alive against their will.'

'It's not against their will!' Callie could have run now, but she stayed to argue, rubbing her arm. 'They're all fit enough to enjoy life. The Colonel says it's wrong to take life from an animal while he can still use it.'

'A crime against Nature.' The Louse was obviously echoing his father. 'Shouldn't be allowed.'

'We save horses! We saved your horse because you were all too cruel and stupid—'

Lewis pulled back his arm and took an open-handed swipe at her, and she ran, ducking through the bushes until she was out on the road where there were people.

When she got home, she kept her sleeve down over her bruised arm and explained her scratches by telling her mother that she had got off the bus half-way up the hill for exercise, and taken a short cut through the brambles.

She told the Colonel that the Pinecrest Hotel had been refused a licence to run a riding stable.

'Thank God,' the Colonel said. 'There is some sense to the Town Hall after all.'

'I'll bet they wish they could put you out of business too.' Callie watched his face to see how he would take that.

'Oh, I don't think so.' In spite of all the cruelty and ignorance he had seen in his work for horses, the Colonel still believed the best of people, right up to the time when he discovered the worst.

'And I've decided,' Callie told Anna and the Colonel – the pain of her arm kept reminding her – 'that I do want to go away to that school.'

'Your name's still on the exam list,' Anna said. 'I didn't keep asking Miss Crombie to take it off every time you changed your mind.'

'Suppose I don't get the scholarship?'

'Miss Crombie thinks you have a very good chance.'

II

One of the disastrous things that people did was to give their small children day-old chicks for Easter. Dear little fluffy yellow Easter chicks. You could buy them in cut-price stores.

Some of them fell out of the paper bags and were stepped on or run over in the crowded street. Some of them were crushed to death by hot little hands soon after they got home. Some died of cold. Some died of the wrong food. Some died of not bothering to live.

The few who survived were either given away when they grew into chickens, or kept in a cellar or a cupboard, or even the bath, until the people got sick of it and gave them away or killed them, or the chickens got sick of it and died. It was a total disaster for all concerned.

This Easter, a town family had staged an even bigger disaster.

Their little daughter was 'mad about' horses, and so when she woke up on Easter morning, the car was standing in the road and there was a horse in the garage.

It was not much of a horse. The family had bought it quite cheaply at a sale. It had a big coffin head, lumps on its legs, a scrubby mane and tail and large flat feet that had not seen a blacksmith for a long time.

'My horsie!' They had bought an old bridle with the horse, and they put it on back to front with the brow band where the throat latch should be and the reins crossed under its neck, and the little girl climbed on, rode away down the middle of the road and fell off before she got to the corner.

She hit her head and was in bed for two weeks, and the horse went back into the garage in disgrace.

Now and then when someone remembered, they fed it a soup can of oats, which it could not chew properly, because it had a long loose tooth hanging at the side of its mouth. It had no hay, because they thought that hay was only for the winter, and no bedding, because they did not know about bedding. There was a small patch of grass behind the garage, and the horse ate that bare, and then licked the ground.

When the little girl was better, she got on the horse again with her friend and the two of them rode round and round on a patch of waste land, clutching the mane and each other and shrieking with joy. Finally, the horse stumbled and fell down, and the children tumbled off, which seemed the easiest way to get down, and a great joke too.

The floor of the garage was concrete and the walls were concrete blocks, sweating a chill damp. When the horse lay down, which it did more often as it grew weaker, it rubbed sores on its elbows and hocks.

If it was lying down when she came home from school, the little girl would get it up by holding the soup can of oats a little way off. When it stood up, she would take the oats away and put on the bridle.

'Work before food, Rusty dear,' she would tell it, and she and her friend would take Rusty to play circus on the piece of waste ground.

She was devoted to the horse. She sang to it. She made daisy chains to hang on its ear. She brushed it with her old hairbrush, but she could not get it very clean, because she did not like the smell of manure, and so she did not clean out the garage, although she told her father she did.

Her father hardly ever went to look at the horse, but he was very proud about it, and told everyone at work how his little girl thought the world of Rusty and it would do your heart good.

The mother did not look at the horse very much, because she was afraid of horses, and said she was allergic to them, which she thought was quite a grand thing to be, and she also did not like the smell that was accumulating in the garage.

But her little girl was happy, and she thought it was a lovely thing for a kiddie to have a faithful pet.

The faithful horse was willing enough to keep going somehow, although he was very thin and lumps of his hair fell out, and he was becoming dehydrated from only having small amounts of water, which the little girl brought him in a seaside toy bucket.

One day when she and her friend were riding him proudly down the road to the pillar box, slapping his ribs to keep him moving, he stopped and lay down in the road with his nose resting on the kerb. All the shrieks and wails and kisses and smacks of the children and the shouts of some masons who were building a wall and the advice of housewives who came out of their houses and flapped their aprons could not get him up.

It happened that the Colonel and Anna were taking a detour across the end of this road to avoid rush hour traffic. They saw the excitement, and turned the car up the street to see what it was.

The Colonel walked through the small crowd and stood for a moment with his hands in his pockets, watching the little girls swarming round the horse like distressed bees, patting it and kissing it and begging it, Rusty dear, to get up. The Colonel looked at the horse and the horse looked at the Colonel, and a message passed between them like old friends.

When the Colonel had got authority to take the horse, he telephoned for Steve to come with the horse box.

'But I don't understand.' The mother had taken the little

girl home and the father was back from work and standing nonplussed in the road, where street lamps were coming on and the masons had knocked off for the day and the housewives and the other children had gone indoors. 'She loved that horse like her own brother. Thought the world of him, it would do your heart good.'

'I'm sorry.' The Colonel was sitting on the kerb in his best suit with the horse's head in his lap. 'But a small child can't be left alone to take care of a horse.'

'But we didn't know!'

'Famous last words,' the Colonel muttered. 'People who don't know anything about horses should stick to goldfish.'

'That's a good idea.' The man began to cheer up. He was glad he was going to be able to garage his car again, anyway. 'I'll get her a bowl of nice fish tomorrow. Take her mind off it. They soon forget, the kiddies.'

He went back to tell his wife and daughter the new idea. The Colonel took off the jacket of his best suit and laid it over the rump of the horse, who lay like a heap of roadmenders' sand in the shadows between the street lamps.

At the Farm, the Colonel pulled out Rusty's loose tooth by rubbing the opposite gum to make that side more sensitive, and then quickly tapping out the tooth with a small hammer.

'Bran mashes now?' Steve let go the bluish tongue, which he had been holding out to the side to keep the horse's mouth open.

'Give him anything he'll eat, if he'll eat.' The Colonel got up from the straw where Rusty was lying. 'He hasn't got much longer.'

'Will he die?' From the doorway, Callie saw the horse through a glittery haze of tears.

The Colonel nodded. That was the message that had passed between him and the horse in the road.

I am dying.

You shall die in peace.

12

Lewis went back to bullying the younger ones, and Callie kept clear of him. If she could keep out of his way until the end of term, she would be safe and free.

The week before she was to take the scholarship exam, she went early to school for some extra study with Miss Crombie. 'Not that I want to lose you next year, Callie, but I shall be thrilled if you do well.' Miss Crombie flushed and scratched her head with the pencil she wore through her hair like Madam Butterfly. She had a pretty boring life and not much to be thrilled about.

When Callie was in the cloakroom, she heard shouting in the yard outside, and running feet. The bigger boys never came so early, but there was a pack of them, galloping across the empty yard like hounds after a fox. She could not see what they were chasing, but whatever it was had dashed into the bicycle shed and bolted the door.

Whooping and shrieking, the boys attacked the shed with feet and stones and bits of wood. One of them broke a window. It was Lewis, of course, climbing on the bicycle rack and putting in the boot with a crash of glass.

Callie watched, paralysed. She had heard about a girl in New York being stabbed in the street while people hurried past or watched from their windows, and would not do anything to help. Now here she was, just as cowardly herself. *Don't get mixed up. Keep clear.*

Lewis was too big to climb through the window. He and the others went round to attack the shed from the back. As Callie heard the glass of the back window break, the door of the shed burst open and a little spindly boy, legs going like the spokes of a wheel, ran for his life across the yard. The boys were already round the shed and gaining on him as he wrenched open a door and got inside the school.

Help him, Callie. But she could not move. The boys were at the outside door as the little boy rushed into the cloakroom, gasping and wild-eyed.

'They're after me!' He could hardly speak.

Don't get mixed up. Keep clear. 'I can't – this is the girls'—' she began, but the child stammered, 'Save me!' and without thought, she pushed him into her open locker and shut the door.

It locked automatically. It was a tiny space, but the child was tiny, and there were air holes at the top to let out the smell of hockey boots and gym shoes.

Feet clattered on the stone stairs, and Lewis was in the cloakroom with three or four grinning cannibals behind him.

'Well, look who's here.' Lewis began to throw coats and scarves about, looking for the little boy.

'Get out of here.' Callie held herself tense so that the trembling of her body would not reach her voice. 'You're not allowed in here.'

'Who cares?' Lewis began to try the doors of the lockers, pulling out stuff from the open ones, while his mob tore clothes off the hooks and threw shoes and tennis rackets about, just for the mess of it.

'Where's that mucky kid?' Lewis was looking through the air holes of the lockers. What would happen when a pair of terrified eyes met his? What would happen when he saw it was Callie's locker and went at her for the key? It was round her neck on a string. He would probably strangle her.

'What's he done?' If she could just keep them talking, someone would come.

'Croaked to a teacher. Got us in trouble.' A gym shoe, a

purse, a stuffed bear flew out of a locker over his shoulder.

'Why?'

For answer, he tore the photograph of a boy from the back of a door, crumpled it up and threw it in her face.

He was getting near her locker. Her hand went up to the key string at her neck. 'There's no—' she said, 'there's no one—'

'Shut up.' Lewis took hold of Callie's long pigtails, wrapped them round her throat and pulled the ends.

Choking, Callie looked desperately out of the window. Then she saw a miracle, right before her anguished eyes. Big bold Betty Rundle, goal for the hockey team, was rolling in early across the yard. The boys saw her too. Lewis let go of Callie's hair, and they ran. Coughing, Callie pulled the child out of her locker, and dragged him – he could hardly walk from cramp – down the corridor and round a corner before Betty Rundle kicked open the outside door and came whistling down the stairs.

Miss Crombie was angry, puffed in the face. 'What's the point of me getting here early if you can't bother to come early too?' She was never at her best in the morning.

'The bus was late,' Callie said faintly. Her throat still hurt.

'It's for your sake, not mine', Miss Crombie went on without listening. 'Now hurry up and let's go through that French translation before the pagan hordes arrive.'

While she read aloud, misreading some of her own words so that they sounded like mistakes, Callie thought about the little boy as she had left him sitting alone in his empty classroom, sheltering behind an oversize desk as if it was a fortress. After he had told the teacher about his books being thrown in the pond, Lewis had lain in wait for him one morning last week and bent back his fingers behind a bus shelter. That was why the boy came to school early.

'But not early enough for *him*,' he told Callie.

His name was Toby. He was about ten – no one at home remembered his birthday – but undersized, with weak, skinny legs and a large shaggy head on which his ears stuck out like the handles on a porridge bowl. He was a weird-looking child, like a goblin changeling. Callie hoped she would not get mixed up with him again.

'Don't leave me,' he had said, when she put him into his classroom.

'Oh, look. I only hid you to save my own skin.'

'You live up the hill, don't you?' His pointed, big-eyed face was like a marmoset. 'So do I. What bus do you get home?'

When she told him, he said, 'I'll wait after my last class and go with you.'

'Oh, look.' She did not want to get *mixed up* with this child.

'I'd be safe with you, see?' Sitting at the desk that was too big for him, he had nodded confidently, as if Callie was as big as Betty Rundle, and as bold.

He was waiting for her. He waited every day and chattered by her side on the bus. In the morning, he was on the early bus, with his face unwashed and his socks in holes on his dangling legs, his books on the seat to keep a place for her.

He chattered while she was trying to read, telling her things about his home and his cats and his brothers and sisters who were bigger than he was – even the younger one – because he had been ill.

'They gave me up for dead,' he said cheerfully. 'I heard them say so in the hospital.'

The exam was only two days away. Callie swotted all the time.

'Why are you always reading?' Toby asked her when she only grunted at his twentieth question about the horses at the Farm, which fascinated him.

She told him about the scholarship. 'If I get it, I'll be out of this rotten school next term.'

Toby said nothing. This was so unusual that Callie looked at him. Tears stood in his big eyes, and his mouth drooped at the corners.

Why should she feel guilty? It was her life, not his. But she did. Before they got to the top of the hill, she told him he could get off the bus with her and see the horses.

Steve was very nice to Toby. He picked him up so he could see over the half doors. He took him on his shoulder out to the fields and let him open gates and hold them for horses coming through. When Cobbler's Dream came in, he put a saddle and bridle on him and let Toby ride in the jump field.

On the ground, the child was topheavy and misshapen, but on the pony, he did not look odd at all. He sat well by instinct, held the reins the way he was told, and learned the rhythm of rising after Cobby had trotted carefully round a few times on the lunge rein.

'Never seen anyone get it so quick.'

Toby grinned with his mouthful of bad teeth. When Steve lifted him down, he clung to the chestnut pony's neck, went into the stable with him, pressed his big head to his strong chest while he was eating, and had to be prised away by force for Steve to take him home.

Callie went with them. Toby lived in a tumbledown sort of cottage with thin prowling cats and decrepit vegetables and a collection of rubbish and old cooking pots and broken furniture outside, as if there had been a fire.

His mother came out, holding a baby which was dribbling at the mouth and nose. 'Where the hell have you been?' Her voice began to lash at Toby before he had opened the gate, lifting it creaking on its one hinge.

Steve explained. The mother still looked grim, partly because she had not got her teeth in.

'He can come back any time,' Steve said.

'We'll see,' the mother said ungraciously.

Next morning on the bus, Callie was reading history.

'I hope you get bottom marks in everything,' Toby said.

'I'll die if I do.'

'I'll die if you go away,' he said, not in sorrowing self pity; just as a statement of fact.

When the examination came, it was like preparing a horse for a show. There was a special supper the night before. Callie washed her hair and cut her toenails and went to bed with hot milk. Her mother was up early to cook her a big brain-building breakfast, and everyone came from the stables to say good-bye – 'As if I was going to my execution.'

Toby behaved as if she was. 'This is my worst day,' he kept saying. 'This is the worst bloody day I ever had in my whole life.'

When Callie left him at his classroom, where she always had to take him because of Lewis, she said, 'Wish me luck,' but Toby only looked at her as if she were a traitor.

'Good luck!' Miss Crombie patted her on the back outside the examination room. 'I know you can do well.'

And when Callie saw the first paper, she knew she could too.

Waiting to see exam questions is one of the worst times in life, doomed, sick, your brain empty of everything you ever learned. The papers are passed out. You turn them over. Your eye scans quickly down and you see, yes, yes, one after the other, things you know, things you have revised, favourite things – two you never heard of, but there's enough choice without them – and then it is your day.

It was Callie's day. She picked up her pen, squared her elbows, smiled at the invigilator, who did not smile back for fear of cheating, and wrote her name beautifully at the top of the beautiful clean paper. *Question No. 1: Name the 6 wives of Henry VIII and say what you know of each.*

Easy, easy. Katherine of Aragon, Anne Boleyn, Jane Seymour, Anne of Cleves, Katherine Howard, Katherine Parr. She knew them backwards in her sleep.

She began to write: '*Katherine of Aragon, Anne Boleyn, Jane Seymour . . .*'

The image of Toby's face, pinched, pale, grubby, the big marmoset eyes and the pointed chin, lay on the white sheet of paper.

'*I'll die if you go away.*'

Callie sighed, crossed out her first words, and began to write again:

'*Katherine Taragon, Ann Seymour, Marie Antoinette, Katherine the Great, Bloody Mary, Katherine Dubarry.*'

No one could understand it. They called it bad luck, an off day, stage fright. Miss Crombie was upset enough even to call her stupid.

'You *knew* most of those questions. They were tailor-made for you.'

'I lost my head.'

'And lost the scholarship.' Miss Crombie was bitterly disappointed.

'I don't really mind. I never did want to go to boarding school.'

'*I* mind,' Miss Crombie said. 'And I mind for your mother.'

'She didn't really want me to go away.'

13

Toby said, 'I knew you wouldn't get it. But I'm glad you didn't.'

Callie did not know whether to be glad or sorry. She had thrown away her chance – but was it worth it? At school, there was not much she could do to help Toby. It was actually worse for him to be the friend of someone whom Lewis hated as much as he hated Callie.

Once when he tripped Toby up in the corridor, Toby managed to bite him as he scrambled up. The Louse had teeth marks on his hand.

Callie saw them, and jeered. 'He's got rabies, didn't you know? Ooh look – you're foaming!' and ran into the crowd.

Toby came quite often to the Farm to ride. Cobby could be a bouncing, jet-propelled handful when Steve got him on his toes to jump, but he was clever enough to know when to take quiet care of a rider. He had once worked for a paralysed girl, walking by himself into a pit so that she could heave herself from her wheel-chair on to his back.

Riding David, Steve took Toby along the top of the hills, through woods and fields and ferny lanes where he had never been before, because his legs would not carry him far. Colour came to his cheeks and his muscles grew stronger. Even his mother, who never admitted optimism, was forced to say that it might be doing him good.

One evening when Callie brought him back to the Farm, he said he could not ride.

'I hurt my hand.' He had it in the pocket of his droopy shorts which were handed down from someone bigger.

'Let's see.' Steve took out the hand.

'Nothing much.'

Steve gently unwound a blood-soaked handkerchief. The nail of one finger was torn off down to the quick.

'Why didn't you go to the nurse?' Anna asked, when she was cleaning the finger and bandaging it.

'I dunno.' He kept his eyes down.

'Did Lewis do that?' Callie asked.

'Who's Lewis?' asked her mother.

'That boy from Pinecrest. You know. The one who is our enemy because of Miss America, and the stable licence. He's Toby's enemy too.'

'Surely he wouldn't do a thing like that to a little boy?' Like her husband, Anna had an enduring faith in human nature, sometimes ill-founded.

The day when he was chased like a small animal, running for his life into the bicycle shed, had taught Toby not to tell tales to grown-ups. But he told Steve how Lewis had caught him on one of the swings and twisted it, jamming his finger between the chains.

Next day, when Steve had finished the morning work in the stables, he went down the hill to the school.

Callie had told him that some of the big boys went down to the end of the playing fields for a smoke after lunch. Steve hid in the bushes, rubbing his knuckles.

Half a dozen boys came down and lounged about for a while, talking in grunts and guffaws, making grubby jokes about the teachers. Steve recognized the Louse's voice, oozing thick and stupid through his adenoids.

Steve crouched, then suddenly leaped out and grappled with him. Surprised, Lewis went down, and they rolled over and over, punching and kicking and scratching and hurting each other in any way they could.

As Steve had expected, the other boys were too yellow to

join in. They watched for a while, circling the desperate fight like dogs. Then when Lewis began to scream as Steve was on top of him rubbing his face into the ground, they ran off.

Cursing, his face smeared with earth and blood, Lewis somehow scrambled up. Before he could get away, Steve caught him with a fist on the side of the jaw and the Louse went down like a felled tree.

Steve wiped his face on his sleeve, rubbed off his hands on the grass and ran them over his curly hair. He found a piece of paper in his pocket, and left a scribbled note tucked behind the ear of the snoring boy.

'You want more of the same? Try starting anything else with the little kids.'

14

Nothing happened for a while. The Louse was away from school for the rest of the week. Steve had a scratched face and a lot of bruises and Callie got up very early, did all his stables for him and brought him a mug of tea in bed.

The grey stable cat had three kittens. They were keeping the prettiest one with the Elizabethan ruff of white fur round its face, and a home had been found for the other two at a village grocery whose storeroom needed the protection of this famous family of mousers.

On Sunday evening, Steve put the kittens in a canvas shoulder bag and rode Cobby to the village, trotting along the side of the road in the gathering dusk.

The grocery people insisted on giving him a snack – he was the kind of boy whom women instinctively fed, not to fatten him, but to mother him – and it was almost dark by the time he started for home.

Dark, light, sunlight, grey shadows, it didn't make much difference to the Cobbler with his half sight, especially on a road he knew so well.

He trotted steadily, ears constantly moving, alertly forward, swivelling back, one forward and one back, because he depended so much on his hearing.

Steve rode half dreaming, the empty bag swinging at his hip. He knew the feel of the pony so well that it was almost like the movement of his own body. He sat relaxed, with a loose rein, not bothering to rise to the smooth trot, fancying himself a cowhand, legs stuck out in chaps, shoulders slack, single-footing through the desert sagebrush behind a herd of lowing cattle, going leisurely to the water-hole.

The motor-bike came out of nowhere, with no light. It threw itself at them round a corner and roared by so close that Steve saw the rider's face in the instant before Cobby reared, slipped on the road and came down hard, with Steve underneath.

His leg was pinned under the saddle. The pony struggled, and at last the weight of him lifted and he was up. Steve did not even try to get up. He did not try to move his leg. He was cold and sweating at the same time, with lead in his stomach and a sick spinning head, and he knew that something was badly broken.

He raised his head to try and look at his leg, lying with the foot at a strange angle, then quickly dropped his head on the ground and kept it there until the blood came singing back into his ears and he knew that he would not faint.

In books when a rider lies hurt on the ground, his faithful horse lowers its head, nosing him gently, and he whispers into its ear, 'Go home!'

In life, things don't work out like that. Cobbler's Dream was a few yards away at the side of the road, his foot through the reins, tearing at the long grass as if he had not had a decent meal for weeks.

Steve whistled to him. He moved on, contentedly grazing. It was almost dark now. Steve could barely see the rounded outline of his quarters, moving steadily away.

No cars came by. Steve's leg had been shocked numb at first, but now feeling was coming back, and with it pain. If a car did not stop soon, he would have to start screaming. If the Louse's big brother came back on the motor-bike to see how much damage he had done, he would have to shout to him for help.

Someone must help. Anyone. Help me. 'Cobby!' he shouted, his face in the long grass.

'Who's there?' A high, nervous voice, some way down the road.

'Help!'

A small dog yapped. Feet on the road. Then they stopped – 'Help!' – came on again. Then a hysterical tongue was licking at his face and Steve grabbed the little dog tightly, in a sweat of panic that it would touch his leg.

'What's happened?' A woman walked round and stood in front of him, staring down, her hand in her mouth. She looked in a panic too.

'I've broken my leg.'

The woman gasped and knelt down.

'Don't touch it!' Steve shrieked. She pulled back her hands and got up.

'I'll run back and get help. I live quite near. You stay there,' she added unnecessarily and ran, feet fading down the road, the dog yapping and yipping as if something marvellous had happened.

Steve closed his eyes and began to groan.

He was in a small hospital in the town where the Jordans had lived among the harassing new neighbours. His leg was in plaster to the thigh. It was very uncomfortable, and 'Yes, it does hurt,' he answered to the question that everybody asked.

The Colonel was furious. He was usually easygoing, a peace-maker; but after what Steve told him, he wanted to steam right down to the Pinecrest Hotel and tell soapy Sidney Hammond what he thought of his rotten, vicious, ugly son Todd.

'No, don't.' Steve closed his eyes. It still made his head ache if anyone raised their voice. 'It was an accident.'

'That's not what you told me when you came out of the anaesthetic. You said it was deliberate. He came at you without lights and practically knocked the pony over. He probably did knock him over.'

'He slipped.'

'What difference?' The Colonel picked up his cap and stick. 'I'm going to tell that two-faced swine—'

'Then he'll tell you what I – what I – oh hell. What I did.'

'What did you do?' The Colonel's voice dropped with a sigh from indignation to resigned patience.

'It was a revenge thing. I'd beaten up his younger brother. You know,' he added hopefully, as if he could persuade the Colonel that he had already heard about the fight, and had not minded.

'I thought you weren't going to get into any more fights, Steve.'

'I can't now.' Steve closed his eyes again and lay like a corpse in a coffin. The Colonel put a hand on his forehead and went away.

15

Steve came back from the hospital with his leg still cocooned in the long heavy plaster, scrawled over with messages from the nurses.

'*Behave yourself – Cathy.*'

'*Good luck from Rosalita.*'

'*Mary Ellen – don't come back.*'

'*Love always Susie*' and a heart with an arrow.

He could move about slowly with crutches. He spent one day sitting in the garden with his radio and various dogs and cats who were glad to find someone sitting still, and Anna bringing him things to eat and drink.

'This is the life,' he told her, but the next day he was out at the stables, trying to do his work again.

'Here, let me.' Dora ran up when she saw him at the outside tap.

'Go away. I am going to be the only man on crutches ever to carry a full bucket of water.'

He settled the crutches under his arms, bent down with difficulty, tried to pick up the bucket and grab the bar of the crutch with the same hand, and lurched forward in a flood of spilled water as Dora caught him just in time.

'Careful.' She propped him up against Ginger's stable. Her face was grave with anxiety, so she quickly smiled. 'That's expensive plaster, you know.'

Gradually Steve found out what he could do. He could carry a feed bucket, hung round his neck on a piece of bailing wire. Then he had to get into a loose box, move the horse out of his way with his shoulder or his voice, prop a crutch against the wall by the manger, unhook the bucket from his neck without the horse getting its nose in and strangling him, and tip the feed into the manger before the greedy horse knocked the bottom of the bucket and scattered the whole lot into its bedding.

He could sweep a bit, and do some grooming, leaning against a quiet horse. He cleaned all the tack, which there hardly ever was time for, and blacked the harness that Cobby wore to pull the blue cart out to the fields. But there was not much more he could do except sit on the old mounting block made out of a milestone (CLXVI miles to Tyburn) and play the guitar to Dora and Callie.

The Shetlands and the donkey had gone back to the children's camp for the summer, and one of the very old horses had died, but five skeletons had come in from the stable of a man who had skipped the country to avoid arrest, and abandoned them. Dora and the Colonel and Slugger had more than they could do.

Steve's plaster would not come off for at least a month, the doctor had said after the last X-ray. So the Colonel rang up the Employment Office and asked for a temporary stable hand.

'I mean a real one. I'd rather have nobody than a damfool girl who gets her big toenail trodden off, or a long-haired layabout who shouts at the horses and goes to sleep in the hay with a lighted cigarette.'

After a few days, Mac turned up. He came in a fairly decent car, but terrible old clothes, a burly man with shaggy hair and a grizzle of growing beard, some age past forty.

'I'm looking for work.' He came rather shyly into the yard. 'They told me to come here.'

'Know anything about horses?'

'Not much.'

'Like 'em?'

'I guess so.' He was American.

'Worked with them before?'

A pause. '*Uh*-huh. But I can learn.'

'References?'

The man smiled and shrugged his shoulders. Under the hair, he had a weathered face, craggy, with the kind of thoughtful, clear-sighted eyes made for scanning far horizons, or searching a face. The Colonel liked the look of him and took him on.

In his dirty old trousers and his yellow-grey sweater that had once been white, pulled out of shape, with loops of thick wool hanging, Mac went straight to work helping with the evening feeds.

There was a storm coming up. You could see it far down the valley, rolling blackly towards the hills, so all the horses were brought in.

Mac pitched hay and carried water buckets, doing what he was told, not asking any questions, not answering any about himself, quiet with the horses, though he seemed to know nothing about them. When Dora said, 'Two on that side need water – the grey and the roan. Know what a roan is?' he thought for a moment, then smiled. 'Sorry.'

When he smiled, his broad tanned cheekbones lifted and his eyes narrowed to a grey glint.

'It's a sort of reddish speckled—' Dora looked at him sharply. 'I've seen you somewhere before.'

Mac shook his head. He had hay seeds in his hair and beard. 'Only in your dreams.'

'What do you think of him?' Dora asked Slugger Jones, as he was leaving for his cottage across the road.

'What do I think? she asks. I seen 'em come, I seen 'em go. Mostly I seen 'em go.'

'I hope Mac stays.'

'Call me Mac, he says, coming out of nowhere. I seen 'em come, I seen 'em go,' Slugger grumbled to no one in particular, clicked his knotted fingers for his terrier and ambled through the archway.

When the work was done, Dora took Mac round to all the loose boxes and told him the names and stories of the horses.

'Cobbler's Dream.' Everyone started with Cobbler's Dream in the corner box. He was so striking, with his bright white blaze, his head always over the door, watching, demanding attention, chewing his hay now, and dribbling it into the yard. Mac picked up the bunch of hay and gave it back to him. Cobby turned his head to observe him with his good eye.

'He was hit in the head,' Dora said. 'Spoiled, stinking brat with a whip. He used to be a champion show jumper. Still could be, even though he can't see much. But we don't go to shows.'

'Why not?'

'We're not good enough. We couldn't afford the clothes anyway. And – oh, I don't know. A horse doesn't mind showing off, but having to perform perfectly, dead to order, our idea not his . . .'

'Maybe he likes it.'

'How do we know?' Dora looked up at him. 'We say a horse loves to jump because he gets all excited, but perhaps he's only nervous. Look at this one – Wonderboy. He belonged to Callie's father, who died. He loved to race, they said, but how do we *know*?'

Mac went 'Hm' into his beard. Dora wondered if she was being a bore.

'I'd love to know what Spot thought about the circus.' She showed Mac the broad-backed apaloosa. 'Three fat ladies in silver wigs and spangled tights danced on him at once, the

Colonel says, though I don't know how he knows, because he won't go to the circus. Anna, his wife, took Callie once and they saw Hero.' She took him across the yard to the brown, ewe-necked horse that Callie had saved. 'His rider was forcing him to lie down, and pulling his head so far round that he couldn't, and then beating him when he didn't. So Callie stole him.'

'How did she get away with that?'

Mac seemed interested. Perhaps he – perhaps he was a thief too? He would tell nothing about himself. On the run? Incognito? The beard looked fairly new and the car was too good for the clothes. If he had stolen that, he'd better get it away from the road.

She showed him the four newcomers – the fifth had had to be destroyed yesterday – the pitiful thin horses which had been abandoned, tied by the head and helplessly starving.

'The owner was some sort of underworld gambling type, who had bought this big house and the horses to make himself look respectable in the neighbourhood. He left in a hurry, he—'

She stopped dead, staring at Mac. What if he—? The thought was into her head and out again in a fraction of a second. She laughed.

'What's so funny?' Mac was frowning at the black horse with the wound on its bony head, shoulders hunched in the awful sweater.

'Fantastic things one thinks.'

'Such as?'

Dora always said what she was thinking. 'I thought for a second, what if you were that man?'

'What would you do?'

'Kill you, I suppose. The halter on this horse was so tight that it was embedded in the flesh. The vet had to cut it out under anaesthetic. Even if it heals, he'll have a dent in his head for ever, like a fossil. All the horses had halter sores. They had nothing to eat. They had chewed all the wood within reach. The one we put down yesterday had started to bite at her own chest.'

'It's unbelievable,' Mac said.

'It's true.'

Dora showed him Fanny, with an empty socket where a drunken gipsy had knocked out her eye, and Ranger and Prince, whose mouths had been cut to bits by the gangs of 'Night Riders', with wire for a bridle. She showed him Pussycat, who had broken down on her way from Scotland to London with a petition for the Queen, the brewery horse and the old police horse and ugly Ginger, who used to have a milk round before the dairy went motorized.

'They were going to put him down, but all the ladies in one street clubbed together and bought him. They call him Peregrine. They think he's beautiful. Do you?'

'I wouldn't know one horse from another,' Mac said.

Heavy drops began to fall out of the sky like lead pellets. The sky blacked over at great speed, like the end of the world. Dora shook back her short hair and stuck out for her underlip to catch the rain. Mac pulled up the collar of his bulky sweater and lowered his beard into it.

Anna ran out, with a coat over her head. 'Come on in!' she called. 'Come in and have some supper,' she told Mac.

'Thanks,' he said. 'I'll get something. I have to go find a room.'

'You can stay here.'

'Thanks.' He backed away. 'I'll be O.K..'

The rain suddenly came down like a waterfall. He ran, splashing to his car.

Anna ran with Dora back to the house.

'What's he afraid of?'

'I don't know,' Dora said. 'I don't think we'll see him again.'

16

He was back in the morning.

He worked steadily and well. He came on time. He left late if there were extra things to do. He became part of the Farm.

After a while, he gave up his lodgings and came to live in the little room behind the tack room.

There was room for him at the farmhouse, or across the road with Slugger Jones and his wife, but he preferred the stuffy little room, which was built into one side of the stone arch, and smelled of leather and horse nuts and his pipe tobacco, and the soups and stews and beans he cooked up on a small stove.

Anna would gladly have fed him, but he wanted to be alone. He was nervous among a lot of people. When visitors came, he got busy in the barn or out in the fields. Sometimes he talked to Steve or Dora or Callie, telling very little about himself, and that little different each time.

He said he had been in gaol, been in the Army, been at sea, been to Australia, lost everything in a flood, lived under the ice in the Antarctic for two years. He threw out bizarre bits of information as if he did not expect to be believed, and nobody believed him.

He still said he knew nothing about horses, but he was naturally good with them, and seemed to like being with them better than people. The Colonel thought he might have been a ranch hand once. There were days when he walked like a cowboy, and when it rained he wore an old hat he found in the barn, tipped over his eyes like a ten-gallon Stetson.

Besides the car, he did not seem to own much. He had very few clothes, a few paperback books, but no photographs. No pictures at all of anybody who belonged to him.

'Haven't you ever been married?' Callie asked him. She and Toby were the only ones who were allowed to come into his room. When the evenings were cool, he sometimes lit a fire in the smoky fireplace and cooked something marvellous in a black iron pot – beans and sausages and molasses and onions and hot pepper ketchup with beer poured in on top. It was much better than supper at the house. They sat on the floor and ate out of the pot.

'Like in the Wild West,' Toby said. 'Was you ever out West, Mac?'

'Listen kid, I been everywhere.' He always said something like that, to stop a question.

'What was it like?'

'Like everything else – loused up.' He always said something like that too.

While they were eating the marvellous beans, he would drink whisky out of a tin mug, and afterwards he would lie down on the low sagging bed and go to sleep. He slept for hours. They had never known a man sleep so much.

Lancelot, an ancient rickety skewbald who had been saved from the fate of being shipped abroad for slaughter, was the oldest horse in the stable. The Colonel judged him about thirty. When Dora or Steve showed him to visitors, they always added a few years to make the people gasp and give him extra sugar. 'Ah, the poor old thing!'

'What's poor about him?' This always disgusted Slugger. 'Life of Riley, he's got. Nothing to do but eat and sleep and make a big mess in his manger.'

You always had to look in Lancelot's corner manger before you tipped in his feed. His front end was fairly strong, but like most old horses, he was getting weak in the loins, so he sat on his wooden manger.

One night the manger went.

Steve, lying stiffly in bed in his uncomfortable plaster cast, heard a splintering crash from the stable. It sounded as if a tree had fallen through the roof.

By the time he had lifted his heavy leg to the floor and groped for his crutches under the bed, the upstairs corridor of the farmhouse was full of running feet. When he got out to the stables they were all there – the Colonel, Anna, Dora and Callie, pulling and pushing at Lancelot who was sitting on the floor like a dog, with his brown and white tail fanned out among the wreckage of his manger.

They finally got him to his feet, where he stood trembling like an old man with ague.

'Once more down like that, and he won't get up,' the Colonel said. 'I'll get Mac to fix a bar across the corner. He can sit on that.'

'Where is Mac?' Steve was leaning on his crutches in the doorway, hating to be only a spectator.

'Fast asleep.' Callie had looked through his cobwebby window. 'The whole place could burn down before he'd know it.'

The surgeon at the local hospital was worried about Steve's last X-rays. The leg did not seem to be mending properly, and he wanted Steve to go to London for a specialist's advice about another operation.

'Over my dead body,' Steve said. 'I'm not going through *that* again.'

'You want to limp for the rest of your life, like me?' the Colonel asked.

'Doesn't seem to bother you.'

'And stiffen up and have to stop riding?' The Colonel had been marvellous in his military days, riding for the Army in international shows, working one year with an Olympic team.

'That damn Toad.' When Steve thought about Todd Hammond and what he had done, he burned with rage, and the palms of his hands sweated with the desire to take him by his stringy throat. 'I should have crippled his lousy little brother. I will too when I get my leg back.'

'I'll drive you to London,' the Colonel said.

Anna went with them, and Callie begged to miss two days of school, so that she could go too.

School was a farce anyway. She had studied so hard for the scholarship exam that the muscles of her mind could not cope with revising for end-of-term exams.

Miss Crombie was very disappointed in her. 'You've gone off,' she said, as if Callie were sour milk.

'What'll I do for two days without you?' Toby put on his pathetic face, eyes very large, mouth drooping, those big bat ears sticking out at right angles.

'Dora is going to take you for a ride.'

Dora was going to ride with him over to the park of the deserted Manor house to show him the famous spiked iron fence which Cobbler's Dream had once so heroically jumped. They started off that evening as the others were leaving for London.

Steve hugged Cobby round his strong arched neck and said good-bye to him, as he always did before he went anywhere. He got into the back of the car with Callie, stowing his clumsy leg away with difficulty, wincing.

Dora and Toby rode out through the archway, Toby with

his head up and his back straight, short legs very correct, his small triangular face split by the smile that would not leave it until he scrambled down at the end of the ride.

'Take care of the Cobbler, Tobe!' Steve leaned out of the car window.

'He's supposed to take care of Toby,' Dora said. 'You care more about that horse than anyone.'

'Why not? He cares more about *me* than anyone else does.'

'Fishing.' Callie pulled Steve back inside, the Colonel crunched his gears in a way almost impossible to do with this car, and they drove away.

Mac was going to drive his car to the park of the Manor house.

'If you'd only learn to ride,' Dora said, 'you could come with us.'

'I'd be too scared.'

'You could ride Willy. Anyone can ride a mule.'

'Except me.'

He followed them slowly in the car along the switchback road at the top of the hill, past the racecourse where some men were staking out enclosures for the point-to-point meeting, and then he went ahead to open the cattle hurdles across the Manor drive so that they could ride in the park.

Because he was watching, Dora showed off a bit with David: slow canters and figure-of-eights with a flying change of lead, turns on the forehand and what she thought was a turn on the quarters. David was well schooled, but he needed a lot of leg and a lot of flexible collection. His figure-of-eights were fast and wide and he was not always on the right lead, but Mac would not know that.

'You see?' Dora pulled the grey horse up in front of Mac. 'It's easy. Isn't he a great horse?'

'Except that he don't always change leads in back as well as in front.'

'How do you know?' He wasn't supposed to have seen that. 'I thought you didn't know anything about riding.'

'Oh, I don't.' Mac had his head under Toby's saddle flap, tightening the girth. 'I guess I read it in a book. I read where it said you should use a lot more outside leg.'

'Well, you read it *wrong*.' Dora pulled David round. Steve was always telling her she did not use enough leg, but she was not going to hear it from Mac, who didn't know what he was talking about.

She took Toby down to the bottom slope of the park where the terrible fence stuck out above the brambled undergrowth, a ditch on the take off, a drop on the other side into the road.

The leader of the Night Riders, trying to escape capture, had ridden Cobby at this impossible jump, not caring if he impaled the pony on the rusty spikes.

Toby and Mac looked at the wicked fence with reverence.

'I could jump that, I bet,' Toby swaggered, but without conviction.

Mac said, 'You'd be crazy to try.'

They went back through the gate to the other side of the fence, where Cobby's rider had fallen and been caught unconscious, with the side of his face split open.

'On that very patch of stones,' Dora said. 'If you look, you can probably still find some teeth.'

Toby got off immediately to look. They let him search for a few minutes, scrabbling among the stones like a miniature grave robber, but it was getting late, so Mac lifted him on to the pony and they went home.

After seeing the jump, which had become a famous legend and was known among local people as Cobbler's Leap, Toby was prouder of the pony than ever. Dora let him unsaddle him and feed him by himself, and he stayed in the loose box, brushing and fussing and trying to whistle through his teeth like Slugger, while Dora and Mac finished the other horses.

When Dora looked over the door, Cobby was still eating.

'How much did you give him? He should be done by now.'

'Just a tiny bit extra.' Toby measured a small gap with the thumb and finger of his birdlike hand. 'Because he was so good.' At home, Toby did not get enough to eat, so to him, feeding was loving.

'Not too much, I hope.' Dora did not go in to check. Toby raised his arms and she lifted him easily over the half-door and carried him out to the car because he was tired.

Cobby went on eating.

17

When they came back from the cottage, Dora felt she had to ask Mac, 'Do you want to come up to the house?' It seemed odd for her to be alone there with all the food, and Mac alone in his little room with perhaps bread and cheese, which was sometimes all he had.

'*Uh*-huh,' he said, and she wished she hadn't asked him. 'I'm going to have a drink and go to bed. I'm bushed. You want a shot of Scotch?'

Dora said, 'No, I hate it,' and felt childish. It would have been more sophisticated to try and drink it.

Her mother had always insisted, 'Have a glass of wine. Learn to drink at home.' Last time Dora went home, her father gave her a glass of water that turned out to be vodka. Dora had been sick.

She went to bed early too, and saw Mac's light go out as she passed the staircase window.

She was woken out of her first deep sleep by a noise from the stables. Banging and thumping, hooves against wood. She sat up. Better go out. What was the good of Mac sleeping out there if he never heard the horses? Poor old Lancelot would have sat all night in the ruins of his manger before Mac woke.

Dora pulled a sweater over her pyjamas and trod into her frayed gym shoes. When she ran out of the back door and down the path, she saw that the lights were on in one block of the stables.

Mac was in Cobby's corner box. The pony was down and groaning, swinging his head about, kicking out at the wall.

'Colic.' Dora went quickly inside.

'Yeah. We've got to get him up.' Mac had a halter on the pony and was tugging at his head. 'Come on, boy – hup, hup! Come on – get up there! Here Dora, you pull this end, I'll try and heave behind.'

They struggled, pushing and pulling, but the distressed pony was as heavy as the great brewery horse.

'I thought you never woke,' Dora panted.

'Couldn't sleep. My past catching up on me. Good thing. If this jughead don't get up, he'll twist his gut and we'll lose him. Try the broom.'

Without questioning why Mac seemed all of a sudden to know what to do, Dora ran for a broom and poked Cobby in the side with the bristle end, trying to shift him. The pony groaned and swung his head round, bumping his nose against his distended stomach.

'Yes, *I know*,' Dora gasped. 'I know what's wrong.' She jabbed hard and the pony snapped at the broom, drawing back his nose from his bared teeth. 'If anything happens to you, Steve will – oh Cobby, get *up*!'

'Move over.' Mac pulled back his foot to kick the pony in the ribs.

'No!' Dora kicked Mac herself. 'Don't you know his stomach is full of gas? Don't you know *anything*?'

'Not much,' Mac said mildly. He went out of the box.

All right, she had kicked him. He wasn't much use anyway. She went on tugging at the rope in a hopeless kind of frenzy. Cobby would die. Steve would come back and Dora would tell him about Toby and the feed. Her fault, her fault. She began to scream at the pony, half sobbing.

'Here, let's try something else in his ear besides yelling.'

Mac was in the box, crouching in the straw beside Cobby's head, which was held out rigid, his jaw set against the tug of the halter rope.

'Hold him like that – tight.' Mac had a tin mug in his hand. He caught hold of Cobby's ear and quickly poured something into it. In a moment, Cobby was up, struggling and staggering, tossing his head and agitating his ear, furious, distressed, distended – but standing up.

'Warm coffee.' Mac emptied the mug into the bedding. 'Learned that from an old horse thief out in Nevada.'

For the rest of the night, they took turns walking Cobby in the yard. He was no better. They had to keep him moving. When Dora telephoned the vet, his wife said he was out with a foaling mare. He would come as soon as he could. No idea how long.

They had tried everything. Colic drench. Liquid paraffin. Huge dose of aspirin in Coca Cola, most of which went down Dora's sleeves as she held up the pony's head. When he would not walk, she went behind him with a broom. He was still in pain, nipping, cow kicking, swinging his head about like a club. He would lie down if they let him.

'Will he die?' Dora had accepted that Mac really did know what he was doing.

'Maybe.'

'We can't – oh Mac, *do* something!'

'Try one more thing.' He gave her the rope and ran across the yard to his room. When he came out, he had one of his flat pint bottles of whisky wrapped round with sticking plaster.

'Hang on to him. Don't want to lose any of this.' They backed Cobby into a corner, Dora got hold of his tongue, and Mac poured all the whisky down his throat.

18

When Steve came back, Cobby was his old self. The whisky had begun to shift the painful blockage in his intestines almost at once.

'Mac saved his life.' Dora said. 'Why did he pretend to know nothing about horses?'

'Perhaps he was a groom, and got sacked for drinking.'

After the heroic night, Dora tried to get the lonely man to talk to her.

'If you can talk about things, they aren't half so bad,' she said.

'They aren't bad,' Mac said. 'Go away Dora, there's a good kid, and leave me alone.'

'At least come for a ride. Do you good. I don't believe any more that you can't ride.'

'I don't want good done to me. I want to be let alone.'

'I came to see if you wanted to go to the cinema.'

'You joking?'

'Why?'

'I already told you. I hate the movies.'

'There's an old Cosmo Spence film on. He's good.'

'Big deal.'

Dora went to the cinema with Callie and they sat through a rather dated film made several years ago, about a Centurion of ancient Rome who rode thousands of miles bareback, looking for his girl friend who was carried off by barbarian hordes. As usual in a Cosmo Spence film, the horse part was the best. He rode a big creamy Arab and performed incredible feats of horsemanship.

'He does all the riding,' Callie whispered to Dora in the dark. 'No stunt man.'

'How do you know?'

'I read it in a magazine. That's how he got famous. After all, he's not that good at acting. You don't need to be if you look like that, the magazine said.'

'You don't need to be if you can ride like that.' Dora watched the screen enviously.

The last point-to-point of the season was late this year, because there had been epidemics of coughing in several stables.

Part of the course was over Mr Beckett's land. He went wild if one of the Colonel's horses was on his property, but the races were different. He got paid, and they didn't go over his vegetables or his seedling fir trees.

At one point, the course ran past the Farm's bottom pasture. You could sit on the fence and get a grandstand view of the horses coming over the brushwood jump at the top of the hill, galloping down to make the turn at the flag, then slowing through the plough to the stone wall, and on to the turf again and out of sight behind the wood. After the second time round, you could run up the hill, through the hedges where the first two jumps were, and into the crowd along the main part of the course to see the finish.

It rained all day. It always did. This course was known as The Bog. But everyone at the Farm went to the races, except Mac, who had begun to drive off somewhere in his free time instead of staying in his room and sleeping.

He had been gone every afternoon last week. They thought he had a girl friend, but no one knew who or where, and no one asked him.

After the second race, Callie and the Colonel stayed at the top of the hill to see the next lot of horses come into the paddock. None of them were special, except a big bay who walked with his groom as if he owned the ring of turf, catching at his snaffle, tail swinging, splendid muscles moving under his shining hide.

'That horse of Dixon's looks well,' the Colonel said. 'I think I'll put something on him.'

'Don't waste your money, Brigadier.'

He turned and saw smiling Sidney Hammond at his elbow, all his teeth on show, a sporty black and white check cap pulled over one eye to make him look like a shrewd judge of horse-flesh.

'That liver chestnut there. That's the one.'

'That weed? It couldn't run water.'

'Make no mistake, Brigadier.' Mr Hammond winked with the eye that was not covered by the check cap. 'You've got to know the inside story on these nags.'

'I do, with a lot of them,' the Colonel started to say, but Mr Hammond had taken his race card and was marking horses in other races that 'couldn't lose'.

To get away from him, they left before the jockeys came into the paddock. As they went towards the line of bookies under their dripping coloured umbrellas, Callie said, 'If he did know anything, he'd give you all the duds.'

'He seems friendly enough.'

'Make no mistake, Brigadier.' Callie looked up at him and winked. 'He'd put you out of business, if he could. The Louse said so, and I believe it.'

They went back to the pasture fence and watched the big field of horses come over the thick brush fence in a bunch, riders leaning back for the drop on the slope of the hill.

Blue with white cross, red and yellow spots, orange with green sleeves and cap. The colourful thunder of them was gone too quickly, crowding round the flag and spattering away through the sticky plough.

'Dixon's horse is going well.' The Colonel had his field glasses up. 'Anyone else have anything on him?'

No one answered. They were all staring after the horses.

'I said, "Anyone—".' The horses disappeared over the wall and behind the wood. The Colonel lowered his glasses and looked round. 'What's the matter?'

'Didn't you see?' Callie spoke at last. 'That man on the weedy liver chestnut, with the gold jacket and blue cap?'

'It fell back there, through the plough. I knew in the paddock, it—'

'But didn't you see? It was Mac.'

When the field came round the second time, Mac was far behind, the liver chestnut black with sweat, nostrils wide and scarlet. It heaved itself through the brush rather than jumped, landed with its head low, and was held together cleverly by Mac's hands and balance.

When he got to the plough, he pulled up and turned the horse. He rode slowly back, reins loose, slumped in the tiny racing saddle in the gold jacket that was too tight for him, the blue silk-covered helmet clamping down his thick hair, the chin strap round his beard. He looked more like a trick motor-cyclist than a jockey.

'Hi there,' he said, as he came nearer.

'Good race,' the Colonel said politely, 'as far as it went.'

'He's not half fit, but this friend of mine had a good sale for him if he ran well. Broke his collar bone last week and couldn't ride, so he asked me to help out. Some help.'

'He's not a stayer,' the Colonel said, 'but you got him farther than most people could.'

Mac laughed. 'I was practically carrying him.'

They were having an ordinary horsey conversation as if nothing strange had happened.

With his tacky old raincoat over his muddy borrowed silks and boots, Mac came up to the house for a long hot bath. He stayed for supper, but left before the end of the meal. He did not say any more about the race, and no one asked him, although they were bursting with the need to ask him many things.

When he had gone, the Colonel said, 'You know, he does look slightly familiar, under all that face foliage. He rides like an old hand. Perhaps he's a trainer, who got ruled off for dope or something.'

'I think he's had some tragedy.' Anna said, 'and has come here to forget.'

'Perhaps he's a murderer,' Dora suggested.

'A spy,' said Steve, and Callie said, 'Perhaps he fell out of a train and lost his memory.'

Mac did his work. What difference did it make?

Except that now that they knew he could ride, he started to ride David. He worked with him every day, schooling him in the jump field, while Dora and Callie and Steve watched and marvelled at what he could do with the grey horse.

'It will add a hundred pounds to his price.' The Colonel was delighted. 'I'm glad I waited to sell him.' Though he would have sold David long ago if Steve and Dora had let him. 'I'm going to start talking about him to some of the dressage people. We should get a really good price for him.'

'Couldn't we possibly . . .' Mac was giving Dora some lessons and David was beginning to go well for her too.

'I need the money,' the Colonel said, 'for these other horses who need us.'

'. . . just for the summer?'

'The barn roof has got to be repaired. I can't afford to keep him.'

19

The Colonel was always hard up. The Home of Rest for Horses was run mostly on gifts of money. Even the people who paid something to keep their old horses here did not pay enough. Sidney Hammond had not paid a penny for Miss America, who was still at the Farm and growing quite fat and leisurely on a life of good grass and no work, a big welt of scar tissue still disfiguring her back.

The price of feed and hay and bedding went up every year. Repairs were expensive. All the gutters needed replacing; they dripped rivulets down hairy old heads stuck out into the rain. The new barn roof would cost far more than the sale of David would bring.

The Colonel would soon have to talk to the Finance Committee. He hated to do that as much as they hated having to hear him.

And so when the continuity girl walked into the yard one day and asked the Colonel if he would ride in the Battle of Marston Moor for a historical film they were shooting locally, the Colonel could have cried, because of the money she offered.

He laughed instead. 'Me? Ride down the side of a gravel pit and jump a stream with a wounded man across my saddle? Good God, no. It would kill me.'

'But I heard you were the finest rider round here. Olympic team and all that.'

'Oh, I could ride a bit in my day.' The Colonel screwed up the side of his face, as he did when he was embarrassed into modesty. 'But that's long gone. Damn knee's too stiff. Look at it.' He bent his lame leg as far as it would go. 'Not much more movement in it than that boy.' He nodded at Steve on his crutches, playing hopscotch in the yard with Callie.

The plaster cast was slightly bent at the knee, so that he could sit. He had found that he could sit on Cobbler's Dream, with the plaster leg stuck out with no stirrup. Since the London specialist had said that he thought it would mend without another operation, Steve was taking more chances with it.

'Oh hell.' The continuity girl was small and dark, with a lively manner and bright black eyes. She looked Italian, but her name was Joan Jones. 'I'm sorry.'

'So am I,' said the Colonel. 'I could have paid half my next winter's hay bill.'

'And we could have finished our outdoor shooting this week. We've been on location too long already. We've got to get the battle scenes done before the weather breaks.'

'Marston Moor?'

'Sixteen forty-four.' Callie had hopped over to listen.

'First defeat of the Royalists,' Joan Jones said, to show she also knew a thing or two. 'Michael Fox, who plays Prince Rupert of the Rhine, he's in command of King Charles' men, and when they're routed by Cromwell and that lot, there's no one to rescue this wounded Cavalier, so Rupert does this great bit on the horse to save him.'

'And breaks his own neck,' the Colonel said.

'No.' Callie had studied the Civil War for the scholarship exam. 'Rupert lived for years after they cut off Charles the First's head.'

'You should have told the stunt man that,' Joan Jones said. 'The first time we tried it, he fell off and cracked two ribs and dropped the Cavalier into the water.'

'You didn't tell me you'd tried it,' the Colonel said.

'I wasn't going to until you said you'd do it. We've got just the right place, over the other side of the valley, that marvellous stretch of bleak moorland, and the sudden sheer drop into the quarry. It looks twice as high and steep from where we've got the camera.'

Mac had been working with David in the field behind the stables. He came round the side of the barn, the horse walking relaxed and limber, the man moving easily to David's long swinging stride.

As he came into the yard, one of the puppies ran at him from nowhere, yapping under his feet. David shied violently, and whipped round to bolt off with his head up.

Mac hardly moved in the saddle, just shifted his weight slightly back and somehow controlled the horse and turned him quietly round without appearing to do anything.

'My God.' The continuity girl was standing in the yard, staring at him with her mouth open and her black eyes astonished. 'Cosmo Spence.'

'What? That's one of my staff,' the Colonel said. 'Mac – bring the horse over here.'

'He's the living spit of Cosmo Spence. Same build. The eyes. The lazy, insolent way he sits a horse. Take off the hair and beard and I'd have sworn . . .'

'I've doubled for him,' Mac said, 'in my movie days. I was supposed to look like him, but I think that's an insult to me.'

'He did all his own stunts,' Joan Jones said.

'Says who? He had a good publicity man.' Mac grinned, his teeth very white through the grizzled beard. 'I done a lot of riding for him, back in the States.'

'Was it *you*,' Callie said, 'in *Angel on Horseback*, where the Centurion jumped right over that cart with the oxen and through the tent and out the other side?'

'Yup.'

'And in *Calgary Stampede*, where he was the only one who

could ride the black horse? And in *Blue Ribbon*, where he's jumping against the clock and the flashbulb goes off and the horse crashes through the barrier?' Callie had seen nearly all the Cosmo Spence films.

'Uh-huh. I cracked my ankle doing that, and they had to lift me on and off.'

'Listen,' the continuity girl said excitedly, 'you want to make some big money?'

Mac shook his head. He was not interested in money. He would not even let the Colonel pay him overtime when he worked in the evening, painting doors.

'Pity.' She turned away. 'The Colonel could have used that money, even if you couldn't.'

'What would I have to do?'

'One day's work.' She whipped round at once. 'Ride for Michael Fox. Prince Rupert of the Rhine at the Battle of Marston Moor. Long curly hair and a suit of armour and those floppy boots. The Mad Cavalier, they called him.'

'Michael Fox, that jerk.' Sitting on David, Mac spat on the ground, a bad habit he had picked up in his Western days. 'He couldn't play a Cavalier, sane *or* crazy. Why give a part like that to a guy who can't ride a bicycle, let alone a horse? Why didn't you get Cosmo?'

'Didn't you hear? He had a breakdown. Very bad. His wife walked out on him, and he was drinking. He's washed up, I'm afraid.'

'You are Cosmo Spence, aren't you?' Steve and Dora and Callie had forced their way into Mac's room with a bowl of Anna's chicken soup – rice and celery and onions and big chunks of chicken. You could almost eat it with a fork. They came in quickly before he could stop them, and stood with their backs to the door so that he could not open it and throw them out.

'What do you think?'

'I knew all along,' Callie tried, then shook her head. 'No, I didn't. But when we saw that film, it bothered me all the time. He looked familiar, Cosmo did. I mean, more than just from other films.'

'If I was Cosmo Spence,' Dora said, 'I'd want everyone to know it.'

'That's just it.' He – Mac – Cosmo – sat on the edge of his bed and ate the soup out of the bowl, with the spoon handle sticking up into the side of his beard. 'Too many people *did* know. And they get sick of you.'

' "All these new kids coming up." My agent used to call me every day, long distance, collect, Hollywood to New York – wherever I was. "You got to get a new image. You've got to get another big part or you'll be finished." '

He put the bowl down on the floor, wiped his mouth on a dirty towel and threw it into a corner. 'Television. That stupid Western series with the fat guy and the little black kid, and I'd done three movies in a row that were all stinkers. I was so goddam tired. My wife stayed in New York. She never came on location with me. I rang her every day. I was lonely. I had all those phoney friends, but no one really but Elsa, after our – well, we had a little girl, but she died.'

No one said anything. He had never talked before. Now it seemed as if he could not stop.

'It wasn't the babysitter's fault.' He ran his strong hands through his beard and his thick hair, and dropped them, slapping the edge of the bed. 'We went to a party. She suffocated in her crib. I never went to any more parties after that. I'd never liked them anyway. Horses were the only thing. I had ten one time when I lived in Wyoming. That was – oh,

I don't know – one time when Elsa left me. She always came back after a bit, and we'd start over.

'Then I came over here to talk about a part my agent wanted me to do – lousy part, jolly coaching days, in capes and beaver hats, I'd have looked like hell – and Elsa wrote she'd gone to Mexico for a divorce. I cracked up. All shot to pieces. Nervous breakdown, you know?'

He looked up at them. Standing by the door, they nodded, although they did not know what it must be like to have the very fibres of your being snap, so that you could not cope with yourself, or anyone else.

'Every time I had to talk to anyone, I cried. Hotel clerk, taxi driver – God damnedst thing you ever saw. They were going to put me in a clinic. I ducked off, got on a train to somewhere, got me – room – I didn't even know what town I was in – hid from everybody and let my hair and beard grow, and didn't surface until I was flat broke.'

'Was that when you came here?' Dora asked.

'Yeah. I'd gone to the Employment Office to get work as a builder's labourer, or something, but someone said "Horses", so I scooted straight up here. Glad I did.' He grinned at them.

'Has it – I mean – has it helped?'

'You bet. I think I'm beginning to be real again. I think I'm beginning to be real for the first time in years.'

'Mr Spence, would you mind,' Callie asked politely, 'if we went on calling you Mac?'

He laughed. 'Finest thing I ever heard.'

20

When Mac saw the gravel quarry that the film director wanted him to ride down, carrying a limp man, and when he saw the common grey horse he was to ride, he said, 'Nothing doing. Not on that clumsy screw.'

'The stunt man took him down O.K.'

'And fell off into the stream, man. They told me.'

'It's the best horse we've got. It's trained.'

'I got one back home is better trained. I got one will go anywhere with me, *and* stay up on four feet.'

'Bring it over tomorrow, and we'll retake the close-ups with Michael.'

The Colonel said No. 'Not David. It sounds too tricky. Never mind about the money. It's not worth the risk.'

'There's no risk. I've had him down banks steeper than that. He's as surefooted as a cat. And the stream – I wouldn't have gone near it on that plug they produced, but David isn't scared of water. He'll jump big, and he'll jump clean.'

'Carrying a man across the saddle?'

'It's a little guy. I've seen him. And the armour is made of aloominum. Light as a feather.'

'I don't know.' The Colonel chewed at the skin round his nails. 'It's too far to ride over there anyway, and Steve can't drive.'

'Mac can drive the horse box,' Steve said. 'I want to take the Cobbler.'

'What for?'

'They need some more Cavaliers in retreat. Duke of Newcastle's Yorkshire White-Coats.'

'With a broken leg in plaster.'

'I'll have armour and a big boot over it. They used to ride with their legs stuck out anyway. I get eleven pounds. I'll put it in the collection box.'

'Don't bribe me.'

But the Colonel eventually agreed to let Mac take David, if they wrapped his legs. They took the ankle boots that old Flame used to wear because she knocked her fetlocks with the opposite hoof, and the wardrobe people painted them grey to look like bits of armour.

David also wore an armoured breastplate, jointed armour over his mane, like the back of a shrimp, and another piece over his forehead. The bridle and reins were of wide coloured leather, studded with bright metal. When he stood on the high ground at the top of the quarry, with his head up and his long tail blowing, he did look like a seventeenth-century battle charger. Mac, in armour and boots, with a glossy wig, his moustache curled and his beard greased into a point, looked like a Cavalier.

'But he still looks like Cosmo Spence.' Joan Jones was in the group by the cameras.

'In his better days,' someone said. 'Poor old Cosmo. He's had it completely, I hear.'

'I heard he was dead,' the cameraman said.

The wounded Cavalier, a resigned young man with a chestnut wig and a Vandyke beard, lay on the lip of the quarry, his helmet gone, his face carefully bloodied with panchromatic make-up. The cameras were placed so that as Mac galloped across them, it would not show that he was not Michael Fox, who had already climbed awkwardly on David for a close-up of the start of the heroic ride. Mac was on the horse now, nudging him with his legs and holding him in lightly, to keep him on his toes.

'Action!'

Standing on the roof of the horse box in the road, Callie and Dora and Toby watched Mac wheel David, as Michael Fox had done, make him come up a bit in front, then trample, then off at a hand gallop that would look faster when they ran the film.

Behind him rode a group of Cromwell's Ironsides. The wounded boy lay like a dead doll on the edge of the quarry. The steep drop below him was the only way of escape.

Mac brought David to a stop with all four feet together at what would look like the very edge of the quarry. He vaulted off, heaved the young man on to the front of the saddle, jumped on behind him, and glancing back at his grim pursuers, he pushed David over the edge and slid him down sitting back on his quarters.

They jumped down the last part where the slope levelled out. The stream at the bottom had firm banks, and with his arm round the boy, Mac gave David three strides and he was over, just as he had said, big and clean, and galloping off over the moor to where a scattered band of White-Coats waited at the foot of the low hills.

On the crest of the hill, in silhouette, a boy on a chestnut pony waved a plumed hat to cheer him on, his leg in the plaster cast stuck out on the side away from the camera

Long afterwards, when the film was finally released, Dora and Callie saw it every day for a week.

David was superb, although you couldn't see much of Mac, because when Michael Fox found out it was Cosmo Spence, he made them cut out the bits of film that showed his face.

But on the skyline, Cobbler's Dream was unmistakable, with his head up to the wind and his long mane streaming from his crested neck. On his back, the young Cavalier stood slightly askew in one stirrup, and waved his plumed hat against the sky to cheer on Prince Rupert of the Rhine.

21

It was something to tell at school.

'Our horses are in a film,' Callie said, to anyone who would listen. She did not usually have much to say at school. It was safer to keep quiet, so that nobody could find out what your real self was like, and attack it.

'Our horses are in a film,' she told Rosa Duff, who sat next to her.

'Go on,' Rosa said.

'It's called *The Mad Cavalier*. You'll have to see it.'

'Is it a horror film?'

'No.'

'Oh.'

Toby, who had been born chattering, and had never learned to keep his mouth shut, even when he was teased, boasted to the younger ones.

'My horse was in a film.'

'Your horse. You ain't got a horse.'

'I have then. I ride it.'

'It ain't yours.'

'How do you know?'

'Because I know it ain't.'

'Well, that's all you know then, because it is.'

The arguments scuffled back and forth, as they did every day among the small boys. Toby's story of the film was submerged in a turmoil of arms and legs.

'Break it up, break it up.' Two or three big boys lounged across the playground, pushing through the smaller ones. If you did not nip out of the way, you got shoved aside or knocked down.

'Toby's a film star!' One of the small boys jumped up and down like a frog, pointing at Toby, trying to get on the right side of Lewis Hammond by jeering.

'I ain't said—'

'Better not say nothing.' Lewis pushed his face close up and wiped his horrible nose back and forth across Toby's button nose so hard it made his eyes water.

The Louse swaggered on.

The frog boy was still jumping up and down inanely, jabbing a finger at Toby.

'Toby is a li-ar,' he sang. 'Where is Toby's fa-ther?'

Toby's father was in prison, but he did not think they knew that.

'Shut up!' he screamed, his eyes still watering, from rage as well as pain. 'You think you're so big, but we got a famous film star at our place, so stuff *that.*'

He was at the Farm so much that it was 'our place', just as the horses were 'our horses'.

'Go on.' The boy stood still.

'Who is it then?' The others, who had been running after the Louse and Co., throwing gravel as near as they dared, turned and came back.

'Cosmo Spence.'

'Who's he?'

'Never heard of him.'

'Been dead for years.'

'I'm sorry, I forgot.' Toby told Mac about letting the secret out at school.

'I told you not to tell anyone.'

'Oh, it's all right,' Toby said cheerfully. 'Most of them had never heard of you and the others thought you were dead.'

Instead of cheering him, this upset Mac more than the letting out of his secret.

'You see,' he said. 'I am finished. They don't know me any more, the kids.'

'I thought you didn't want to be known.'

'Only if *I* choose. Not if they choose.'

He was gloomy for the rest of the afternoon, muttering about being all washed up, and giving the best years of his life, and nobody caring.

But towards evening, there was a tremendous noise in the road outside. Three cars pulled up together, and a crowd of screaming women rushed into the yard. 'Where is he? Where is he?'

The schoolchildren had told their mothers, and they had all come looking for Cosmo Spence, idol of their youth.

'Cosmo!' They rushed at him like a pack of yapping beagles.

Dora looked at Mac, and saw that he was terrified. He was pale and shaking, unable to move. She pushed him into a stable and bolted the door.

His fans were streaming through the archway. Dora had been washing down the yard. The hose was still running. She grabbed it, twisted the nozzle to a full jet and turned it on the women.

Their giggling shrilled to screams. They ran, skittering over the cobbles, while Dora stood in front of the stable door where Mac crouched, holding the hose like a fireman, flushing out one woman who had ducked behind a wheelbarrow, and chasing her out after the others, through the arch and into the cars.

'Thanks, pal.' Mac stood up and peered cautiously over the door.

'You still want to be known?'

'No, sir. It brought it all back. The shakes. Geez, I'd be a nervous wreck if I ever had to go to a première again. They tear your guts out. It's terrifying. They eat you alive.'

'Like vampires,' Dora said.

'Yeah. They suck your blood.'

Next morning, they found him in his room, packing the few clothes and possessions that he owned.

'I hate to let you down,' he told the Colonel, 'but after yesterday, I can't stay here.'

'Where are you going?'

'Back to the States, I guess.'

'To Hollywood?'

'No, sir. Being here at the Farm has taught me a hell of a lot. It's shown me the way I want to live. I'm going to get me a ranch somewhere and start a place like this for old horses in the States. Get a couple of good kids to work with me—'

'I'll come,' Callie said.

'Maybe later.' He smiled at her with his very white teeth which had been straightened and capped in his film star days. 'I'll be there a long time, honey. Just another old horse put out to grass.'

22

In the summer holidays, Callie worked harder than she ever did at school, but it did not seem like work. It seemed like the real purpose of living.

With the horses mostly in the fields, there was not so much stable work to do, but summer was a time for repairs and painting and mending fences and trimming hedges and restoring the land. With the money Mac gave him from the film, the Colonel was able to buy a small tractor to plough up part of the pasture, and harrow and re-seed.

In the long evenings, Steve and Dora and Callie rode on the fine springy turf along the top of the hills, or went down to the river, bare-back, and barefoot in shorts. They rode the horses into the water, then tied them up to graze in the lush meadow, while they had supper on the midge-misted bank.

One evening, the Colonel came into the kitchen, where Dora was starting to make sandwiches.

'If you're going riding,' he said, 'don't take David. A chap is coming over to try him.'

'Are you really going to sell him?'

'Dora, I must. I can't have a fit young horse taking up room here. We'll be crowded for the winter as it is, with more coming in.' He went on through into the office.

Dora put down the knife in disgust, threw the bread back into the bin and gave the end of the ham to the dog that was sitting behind her, as a dog or cat always did when anyone worked at the counter.

She and Steve and Callie stayed at home to view this interloper, whom they were prepared to hate.

He was a quiet young man in well-cut breeches and decent boots, with a country face and not much to say. He stood at the door of the loose box and looked at David for a long time without making any comment.

The Colonel did the same. They both chewed a piece of hay. Then the young man went up to David and patted him casually on the neck and murmured to him. He ran his hand down his legs, and picked up a foot, then came back to stand by the Colonel, and they both looked at the horse again.

Horse-trading is a strange, slow, closed-mouthed business. As an old sportsman once wrote:

The way of a man with a maid be strange,
But nothing compared
To the way of a man with a horse
When buying or selling the same.

'Throw a saddle on him?' the young man said at last.

'If you like,' the Colonel said, as if the young man had not come especially to ride David. 'Steve?'

Steve took his time. He went slowly on his crutches, although he was by now quite nippy on them, and carried the saddle back on his head. He brought the worst saddle, and had to be sent back for another. He took a long time tacking up, moving the buckles of the cheekstraps up and down and ending in the same hole, since it was David's bridle and already fitted him. The young man watched. Another unwritten law of horse trading is that you don't help to get the horse ready, even when the groom has a broken leg.

'Go easy with him,' Steve said, as he held the grey horse for him to mount. 'He's very jumpy.'

'Shies a bit, does he?' The young man sat sideways, adjusting a stirrup leather.

'No,' said the Colonel, and Steve said, 'Yes, he shies a lot. He's a very nervous horse.'

He showed him where he could try David, and disappeared. He could not bear to watch.

The young man rode quietly for a while in the schooling ring, hopped over a few jumps, then trotted down the lane alongside the hedge to the big field where he could gallop.

When he was nearly at the gate, Steve suddenly started up the tractor with an explosive roar behind the hedge. David shied violently – any horse would – shot off with his head up, jumped the high gate with feet to spare and galloped off before the young man could collect him.

'That's the end of *him*,' Steve said to Dora behind the hedge.

They worked with the tractor for a while, and when they came back to the house, the Colonel said, 'Chap's coming back for David tomorrow. He's very pleased. He thinks he can make him into an Event horse, when he's worked up his dressage and his jumping.'

They stared. 'Can he handle him?'

The Colonel smiled. 'He should. He was runner-up in the Pony Club Combined Training Finals two years ago. Bad luck, Steve.'

Bad luck because the horse was sold, or because the trick didn't work, or both? With the Colonel, you were never quite sure how much he knew.

At the beginning of August, two girls in a red Mini were driving by and saw the sign on the gate and came in to visit the horses. They were secretaries from London, and they were on their holiday.

'At least, we *were*,' they told Anna, who greeted them, as

everyone else was in the hay field. 'But it's all been ruined this year.'

In answer to an advertisement in a magazine, they had booked rooms at the Pinecrest Hotel.

'*Ride every day*,' they had been promised. '*Fine mounts. Beautiful countryside.*'

'When we got there,' the fair plump one was round all over, with round eyes and round pink cheeks like polished apples, 'the stable was almost empty. Just two skinny old horses, but Jane and I wouldn't ride those poor things.'

'The people were quite nice, but we wouldn't stay. It was the horses we'd come for. They wouldn't give us our money back.' Jane was the dark one with glasses. 'We tried to protest, though Lily and I are no good at doing that, but they showed us a piece in small print at the bottom of their letter.'

She fished in her shoulder bag and showed Anna the letter, which warned in a fine print whisper, '*Deposit not refundable under any circumstances.*'

'Anyway,' Lily said. 'It's too late to get in anywhere else where there's horses. On the way home, we saw your sign and thought we'd just come in. It's the nearest we'll ever get to a horse this summer.'

When Anna had showed them the horses in the orchard and the top field, Lily and Jane helped her to carry cold tea and buns down to the far hay field. Cobbler's Dream was in the shade of a hedge with the cart, and they fell on him with affectionate cries and gentle caresses. They were frustrated horse lovers, who had always lived in the city and could only pat police horses and watch the Lifeguards. While the workers drank tea and rested, they seized hay forks and began to turn the windrows, with more energy than skill.

Anna talked to the Colonel, and then she said to Lily and Jane, 'Why don't you spend your two weeks here? You can have a room with Mrs Jones across the road. Steve won't have his plaster off for another week or two, so you can help us in return for a free holiday. If you'd like to.'

'If we'd like to!' They dropped their forks, prongs up, the way amateurs did, and rushed at her.

23

They were not much use, because they did not know much, but they were sweet and amiable girls, and kept saying that it was the happiest holiday they ever had.

They were never out of bed in time to do the morning feeds. They overturned wheelbarrows full of manure in the middle of the yard. They put horses into the wrong stables. They went barefoot and got their toes trodden on. They ran the lawn mower without oil. They left potatoes on the stove to boil dry. Lily dropped the wire cutters down behind bales of hay. Jane dropped her glasses into the pond and could hardly see. They left a gate unchained, and the Weaver, who was always chewing on things, flipped up the fastener and let himself and Stroller out into Mr Beckett's clover.

Fortunately, Lily and Jane were out for a late moonlight walk with Slugger's terrier. They could never bear to go to bed before midnight. That was why they could never get up.

The little fox terrier squeezed through a hedge and set up a frenzy of barking, which began to be answered by dogs from all round and far away, until it seemed that the whole hillside was awake.

When the terrier would not shut up or come back through the hedge, Lily and Jane ran down the road to the gate and found the Weaver and his friend gorging themselves on the ripe clover.

The girls sat on the gate in the moonlight and thought how nice it was to see the dear old horses enjoying such a succulent meal.

The terrier was still barking, and so were all the other dogs.

An upstairs light went on in Beckett's farmhouse, and then a downstairs light.

'I say,' Lily said to Jane, 'if this field doesn't belong to the Colonel, perhaps we'd better try and move the horses.'

Jane had a belt. They tried to get it round the Weaver's neck, but he always moved just a few steps away. They got it round Stroller, and tugged and entreated and slapped him gently on his broad rump, but his huge feet were planted firmly in the clover and he would not budge.

The belt broke. While Lily and Jane stood and watched the horses and talked about what they should do, they heard Slugger call to his dog from the other end of the field. The dog went to him, and when he saw the horses, he came wheezing up through the field.

'What's this, what's this. Come up, you old fool. Get out of it.'

Although the girls had not been able to get a hand on the Weaver, Slugger went easily up to him, grabbed a handful of his mane and yanked him off towards the gate.

'If them fool women would get behind that dray horse and throw a sod at him, he'd follow,' he grumbled.

'It seems a shame when he's having such a good feed,' Lily said.

'Good feed? They never heard of grass staggers?' Slugger asked the moon disgustedly.

He got the horses back into their own field before Mr Beckett came down the lane in his Land Rover, with his two big dogs in the back, still barking. He saw the trampled clover and the hoof marks and started walking towards the Farm.

'It was our fault,' the girls told Slugger. 'We'll talk to him.'

'Good luck to *them*.' Slugger whistled his dog and hobbled off towards his cottage.

'We're so sorry.' They ran panting up to Mr Beckett.

'It was dreadful of us.'

'We forgot to chain the gate, you see.'

'It won't happen again.'

'Wasn't it lucky they didn't get grass stumbles?'

'Grass staggers, Lily.'

'They did love your clover though. It's a beautiful crop,' Lily said, as graciously as the Queen Mother congratulating a cottager on his tomatoes.

Mr Beckett, with Wellingtons and a raincoat over his pyjamas, stood scratching his bristly grey head as they bombarded him with friendly apologies. He did not know what to say. Even his dogs had stopped barking.

'So please don't be angry, because we're dreadfully sorry we woke you up, but everything is all right now and there's nothing to worry about.'

'I told the Colonel, if his horses got on my land again—'

'Oh, but look. They haven't done any harm. The clover will all spring up again.'

'—I'd shoot 'em.'

'Oh, you can't have meant that, surely.' Lily beamed at him with her polished cheeks, and Jane asked him to come back to the cottage for a cup of tea.

'I've not seen you two before, have I?' Mr Beckett looked at them suspiciously. 'Are you related to the people here, or what?'

'Oh no, we work at the stables. Grooms, we are.'

'We take care of the horses.'

'Oh my,' Mr Beckett said. 'The Colonel must be hard up for labour.'

He went back to his Land Rover, cursed at the sleeping dogs and drove off.

Lily and Jane passionately wanted to ride, but when Dora let them try with the mule, Lily got on facing backwards, and then Willy headed Jane straight back into his stable and almost knocked her brains out on the doorway.

'Oh Willy, that wasn't very nice.' Lily led him out again.

'How could you have ridden every day at Pinecrest if you didn't know how?' Dora asked.

'That was why we wanted to ride every day, silly. We were going to learn. Turn him, Jane! Don't let him run back again. Pull the left strap, same as a bicycle.'

Dora let them fool about for a while with Willy. The long-suffering mule either stood like a rock with one girl on his back and the other dancing backwards in front of him, holding out a lump of sugar, or made sharp rushes for his closed stable door, the feed shed, the hay barn, and finally out through the archway.

Jane shrieked like a train whistle. A man and a boy coming in from the road grabbed the reins and brought the mule back into the yard.

'Going to a fire?' The man laughed at Jane, showing all his teeth.

The lanky boy, with pimples and long greasy hair, stared insolently, sucking his teeth and looking Jane up and down.

'I was going out for a ride, thank you.' Jane dismounted with what would have been dignity if her knees had not buckled at contact with the ground, so that she had to clutch at the man's arm.

'Whoa there, Missy,' he said.

She peered at him shortsightedly. 'I know you, don't I?'

'Should do.' It was Sidney Hammond, proprietor of the Pinecrest Hotel.

'Well, er – excuse me. I've got to go.' Lily had run to the house. Jane left Todd Hammond holding the mule and followed her. Dora had disappeared too when she saw who it was, in case they recognized her as the girl with the pink slacks and Passion Flowers.

She sent the Colonel out to them.

'A pleasure, Brigadier,' Sidney said, pleasantly enough, though his teeth were gritted, rather than grinning. 'I see you've got two of my young ladies up here. I didn't know you'd gone into the hotel business.'

'Who—? Oh them. They're working for me. They had a bit of bad luck, they – oh yes.' The Colonel remembered.

'Two rooms for two weeks.' Mr Hammond said. 'Plus all meals, not to mention what that kind will spend at the bar once they're in holiday mood. That's quite a little loss to me, you will agree.'

'They wanted horses,' the Colonel said. 'It's not my fault.'

'And yet my memory tells me – correct me if I'm wrong – that not too long ago, you gave yourself a little tour of my stables.'

'Oh, that.'

'Yes, that.'

'It was nothing to do with me,' the Colonel protested, but Sidney Hammond held up his hand.

'Please, my dear Brigadier, we'll let bygones be bygones. I'll not hear another word.'

Which was a good thing, since the Colonel was quite embarrassed, and did not have another word to say.

Willy relieved the tension by snapping at Todd, who hit him on the muzzle. The mule spun round and kicked out, as the Toad jumped out of the way.

'You've got to be careful with mules.' The Colonel took hold of Willy.

'Is that why you let those silly girls ride him?' Sidney Hammond asked. 'I hope you've got good Third Party Insurance, Brigadier, ha, ha.'

Miss America was in her stable because of midday flies, and

when the Colonel had unsaddled Willy, he found Mr Hammond and Todd looking at her.

'My mare looks a treat.' He was smiling Sidney again. 'I must say you've done a fine job with her.'

'Thank you.'

'I came to tell you I'll be bringing my trailer up for her tomorrow.'

'I thought you – I thought you'd given up your stable.'

'In a business way, yes. With the money we spent on those horses, we couldn't make it pay,' said slippery Sidney, as if they had never had the conversation about the riding stable licence only five minutes ago. 'But we still keep a few favourites for our own use. My boys are great riders. Beauty Queen will get plenty of work, don't worry about that.'

'That back of hers won't stand any work at all,' the Colonel said, 'the way the scar tissue has lumped up. You put a saddle on it, it will break down again.'

'Oh, I *know*. We just want her as a pet, and I'm going to lead my little grand-daughter about on her. "Grandpa," she says. "Take me for a wide." Of course, she thinks it's riding, though all she does is sit there while I lead her round the path and her Granny snaps her picture.'

It was a beautiful image, except that the Colonel was almost sure he had not got a grand-daughter.

'It came to me what he was going to do,' he said later at supper. 'He was planning to get some horses in again, and get round the licence difficulty by raising the price of rooms to include riding, so that he wouldn't actually be charging for the hire of a horse.'

'Very clever,' Steve said.

'He is cunning. I wish he wasn't so affable with it. I always find myself quite liking him, although I know he's a rat.'

'Rat, Toad, Louse. You should call the exterminators.'

'I told him he could have the mare—'

'Oh *no*!'

'—when he paid the bill. She's been here quite a time. If I charge full boarding fees, he can't possibly pay.'

Everyone applauded him, and Lily said, 'Colonel dear, you *are* clever!' as if there might have been some doubt.

24

Towards the end of their holiday at the Farm, Lily and Jane got restless, and wanted to go into town to dance.

'Dora, you come. Do you good.'

'I can't dance.'

'You can stand in the crowd and twitch,' Jane said. 'That's all there's room for.'

'It's not my style.'

'Perhaps it ought to be,' Anna said. 'Sometimes I worry about whether this kind of life is right for a young girl.'

'You sound like my mother,' Dora said.

'Thank you. Is that a compliment?'

'No.'

The three girls went off on the bus, but they never got to the dance place, or even into town. On the way, they passed a fairground, and it looked so inviting, with coloured lights and blaring music, that they spent the evening there instead.

Dora went on the big roundabout three or four times. It was strange. She could ride a real horse at the Farm almost any day, and yet she could not resist the fascination of sitting astride the cool wooden painted horse, up and down and round and round, all four legs impossibly prancing, nostrils flared, teeth bared, the twisted barley sugar brass pole to lay your cheek against, the crowd and the trodden grass and the upturned faces spinning faster and faster into a blur, the blare and tootle and thump and clash of the pipe organ, swelling and fading and swelling again as you came round past the bosomy figurehead ladies, the painted signs: 'Longest Ride at the Fair', 'Oh Boy!', 'Yes! It's the Galloping Horses!'

When Dora got off, Jane, shooting at random without her glasses, had won a large yellow rabbit at the rifle booth. 'Something for our money at last.'

'What can you do with it?'

'What can you *do* with it?'

What did you have to do with an enormous yellow nylon fur rabbit except keep it on your bed until you got sick of it and stuck it on top of the cupboard to collect dust?

There was another, much smaller roundabout at the end of the fairground, among the 'Kiddies' Rides'. Feeble cars on tracks, with steering wheels which the kiddies turned zealously and thought they were driving. Little boats that floated endlessly round a doughnut-shaped tank of dirty water, while a strong dreamy boy stood in the hole of the doughnut and turned a crank to keep them moving.

The merry-go-round was not turned by a dreamy boy. Instead of painted horses, there were four live ponies, each with a breastplate attached to a bar which turned on the hub as they pottered slowly round and round.

It was not exactly cruel, and yet it was not exactly what a pony ought to be doing.

Dora and Lily and Jane watched for a while. A big man with a simple face and a wobbly paunch lifted the children into the saddles. They rode round a small circle, the bigger ones jiggling and bouncing, or sitting tight, lost in a dream that they were galloping, the tiny ones petrified, staring at their proud mothers all the way round, begging silently to be lifted down.

The ponies were Shetlands with trailing tails, quite well kept. Although Dora and Lily and Jane watched critically, with the narrowed eyes of experts, they could find no cruelty to complain of, except possibly to small children.

But Dora said on principle, as they turned away, 'The ponies hate it.'

'Oh no.' The paunchy man turned round, with a wriggling child in his arms. 'They like it.'

'How do you know?'

Someone in the crowd giggled.

'When I put the harness on, each one walks to his place and stands to be hitched up. Don't you, love?' The pony hardly came up to where his waist would be if he had one. He could have bent over it, if he could have bent, and touched the ground on the other side.

He put the child gently into the saddle, whistled, and the ponies moved forward, little hoofs the size of coffee mugs pockmarking the soft ground. When he whistled again they stopped, and the children were lifted down.

'Not much of a ride for five pence,' Jane said, since there was nothing else to complain about.

The man turned his mild face round to her and said, 'Quite enough for my little ponies.'

The fair was closing when they left. They were waiting at the bus stop, when Jane suddenly cried out, 'My rabbit!' She had left it at the fair, near the pony-go-round where she had put it down to pat one of the Shetlands.

'Come back with me.' She dragged at Dora's arm.

'We'll miss the bus.'

'Anna will come for us. She said she would if we phoned.'

The bright fairground illuminations were out. There were only a few working lamps where people were cleaning up or shuttering the booths, and windows and doorways of trailers spilled patches of light on to the trampled ground.

The yellow rabbit was not where Jane had left it.

'I could have told you.'

'They probably put it back in the rifle booth for tomorrow.'

'I'm going to look. I'd know it anywhere.'

'It's all shut up.' Lily began to walk back.

'My rabbit.'

Going to the gate, they passed a small open-sided tent where the four Shetlands were tied in stalls with canvas partitions.

Lily ran in out of the darkness, and put her hand on a pony without speaking to it. The pony jumped, pulled back, broke its thin rope and made off, ducking and swerving in fright as the three girls tried to catch it.

It knocked over some crates, tripped over a guy rope, skittered round the ticket booth and out into the road, hard little hoofs pattering, with Dora and Lily after it. Jane had fallen over the crates and the rope too and was some way behind.

It was a fairly busy road. The cars were not going fast, but they were coming steadily in both directions. The pony ran along the side of the road, then swerved across the middle. For a moment, it was caught in headlights, outlined all round like a haloed donkey in a Christmas crèche, and then it disappeared in a scream of brakes.

The car skidded, slid into a car coming the other way, and was rammed from behind, just as the first car was hit in the back. The crashing and screeching of brakes and the tinkling of glass seemed to go on for ever.

When Dora and Lily ran up, there were five cars already involved in the crash, and one more just skidding up to bash headlights into tail lights. Screech. Crash. Pause. Tinkle. Car doors opened everywhere and the road was full of people.

'It was the pony,' the first driver kept shouting, waving his arms about.

'What pony?' No one could see a pony. Dora and Lily were on hands and knees looking for it under the car.

They thought it must be dead, but Jane, limping along with her knees grazed and her ankle bruised, met the pony going home head on. She grabbed it by the broken rope and yelled to the others, 'I've got it! I've got the pony!'

If she had not done that, the girls might have been able to slip away and let the people in the cars, none of whom was hurt, argue about hallucinations and bad lighting and blind spots in the road. As it was, the police got the whole story, and the newspaper also got the whole story, slightly wrong.

'RESCUE EFFORT ENDS IN SIX CAR CRASH'

After they explained to the police, Lily and Jane had talked to a newspaper reporter, thinking he was a detective, because he wore a belted trenchcoat with a cape on the shoulders, like old television films.

'We were sorry for the ponies,' they had said. They added, 'But then we saw that the man was good to them,' but the breakdown lorry arrived with a deafening siren as they said that, and the story that came out in the paper sounded as if they had deliberately let the pony loose.

The Colonel went to the owner of the pony and also to the newspaper, to set the story straight, but he got several letters from the kind of people who may never write so much as a Christmas card, but are always moved to write a letter when one of Our Dumb Friends is involved.

Some of the letters were cranky. Some were sentimental. One had a twenty-five pence postal order in it 'to buy the little fellow a bag of carrots.' One was a poison pen letter, unsigned.

'*Why can't you people mind your own business?*' it said. '*Not that your business is anything to boast of, keeping those wretched animals alive that should have been put out of their misery long ago . . . Trying to stop a man from earning an honest crust of bread . . . Should be stopped yourselves . . . We know your sort and what we know we don't like.*'

'What are they talking about – "crust of bread"?' The Colonel looked up. 'Who could have written a thing like that?'

'The man at the roundabout?' Jane suggested.

'Not with that gentle face,' Dora said. 'And the writing is too good.'

'The writing . . . Jane,' the Colonel said, 'go and get me that letter you had from the Pinecrest Hotel. The one that Sidney Hammond wrote.'

The handwriting was the same.

25

In September, when the fruit pickers came to the valley, they brought two ponies up to the Farm for their annual holiday. The Colonel would always take in working horses and ponies for a few weeks of rest. The owners paid what they could, or nothing if they couldn't.

Sometimes, about this time of year, a costermonger's pony or a gipsy horse would be brought in 'for a rest', and the owners would then disappear, so that the horse would be sure of good food and shelter for the winter. They would come back all smiles in the spring, with gifts of firewood and vegetables, and probably be back the next autumn to try the same thing again.

The Shetlands and the donkey were back from the children's camp, and Steve would soon go to fetch the nurseryman's Welsh pony who came every year. His plaster was off now, and the leg mended. He brought a piece of the cast back after they took it off at the hospital, and they buried it at the spot where the motor-bike had ditched him, and Callie drove in a stake, as if it was through the Toad's heart.

An old man wandered vaguely into the yard one day, clutching the newspaper story about Dora and Lily and Jane and the fairground pony.

'I seen about this place in the papers,' he said. 'Touched my heart. I wish I could give you people something for the wonderful work you do, but I'm not a rich man.'

'Who is?' The Colonel had Ranger's foot in his lap, trimming the hoof.

'Got my pension, that's about all it is, and my chickens and goats, just about keeps me going.'

He had watery blue eyes and wispy grey hair over a pink scalp. 'I got an old mare. Hard-working old girl. I'd give anything to give her a bit of a reward for all the years she's given me.' He sighed and shook his head at his turned-up boots, then raised his eyes to see how the Colonel was taking it.

'I'm sure you would.' The Colonel put down Ranger's hind foot and moved round to the other side.

'I seen in the paper that they can come here for a rest.' The old man followed him round, shaky but determined. 'So I came up to ask whether my old girl—'

'I'm awfully sorry.' The Colonel kept his head down, because he hated having to refuse anyone. 'I'm full up at the moment.'

'She can stay out in all weathers. She'd be no trouble to you. I just thought, if I could get her on to some good grass for a month or so, it would mean the world to her.' He paused, and watched the Colonel working skilfully on Ranger's hoof. 'She's earned her rest, mister.'

'Oh, all right.' The Colonel put down the hoof and stood up, slipping the curved knife into the pocket of his leather apron. 'But only for a month. We've got too many for the winter already. Just a month, all right?'

'God bless you, sir.' The old man's eyes swam with emotion. 'And all who work with you.'

But in spite of his shaky hands and his moist, emotional eyes, he turned out to be a pretty shrewd old man. In a neighbour's truck, he brought the mare, and also her treasured companion, a nanny goat in milk, so that the Colonel should have some return for his kindness.

'Who's going to milk it?'

'Not me.'

'Count me out.'

'I'm too busy.'

'I don't know how.'

It turned out that the only person who would milk the goat was Toby, and he managed it very well, sitting on a stool with the three legs cut down to make it the right height, and the goat working on her cud like chewing gum. She was crabby with everyone else but him. He milked her twice a day before and after school.

'Who wants to drink goat's milk?'

'Not me.'

'I hate it.'

'Anna can make cheese with it.'

'I don't know how.'

So Toby took the milk home to his mother, and she gave it to her sickly new baby, who began to thrive.

The goat was out in the fields all day with the mare, making rushes if the other horses came close. The dusty black mare was getting on in years, with battered legs and a long bony head with flecks of white round the eyes like spectacles. Her name was Specs. She had been in the old man's yard for years. She was reasonably fat, but she tore into the meadow grass like a fanatic. After two weeks, someone discovered that she was in foal.

'The old game,' the Colonel said. 'Sneak them in here to have it. But he's not going to get away with it.'

When the old man did not turn up at the end of the month, the Colonel went to the town where he lived and drove round for two hours looking for the address the old man had given him. There was no such address. No one had ever heard of the old man, or his mare, or his goats and chickens, or even his neighbour with the truck.

'He'll be back in the spring,' the Colonel said when he came home, 'for his mare and foal. The old devil.'

But Callie and Toby were thrilled, and so were Steve and Dora. They had not had a foal at the Farm since the Colonel had rescued the mare at Westerham Fair.

Callie took extra care of Specs. The vet said it was a first foal, and she was a bit old for it, so Callie brought her in every night and gave her extra food and vitamins, and came out in her nightdress long after she had gone to bed to shut the top door of the stable if the night turned cold.

They kept her in the separate foaling stable behind the barn, since she seemed to be getting pretty near her time.

'Will you wake me?' She made the Colonel promise to call her if the foal was being born. She had a private fantasy that the old man would never come back, and they would be able to keep the foal. She would call it Folly. Follyfoot, after the Farm. She would handle it and play with it right from the start, so that it would always like people.

'Don't worry,' she murmured into the mare's long furry ear. 'Callie's here.'

The old lady rested on her scarred and weary legs, with her grizzled head low and her bottom lip hanging, ratty eyelashes down over her spectacled eyes. She was not beautiful, but she was content. Her sides bulged like a cow. The Colonel thought it would be any time now, and Callie would hardly risk going to sleep.

On the bus to and from school, Callie and Toby talked endlessly about the foal, planning its future like doting parents. New babies in Toby's family had always been more of a burden than an excitement, but this one was different. He and

Callie could hardly exist through the school day until they could rush back to the farm.

Callie started to ring her mother up half-way through the morning to ask, 'Any news?' Once, at break, she was in the call box at the end of the staff corridor, and she turned and saw a squashed white triangle of nose flattened outside the glass, where the Louse was staring at her. When he took his face away, it left a wet smear.

Callie held the receiver and kept on pretending to talk long after her mother had rung off. But the buzzer went for class, and she had to hang up and come out of the box. Lewis fell into step beside her, quickening his pace as she quickened hers.

'Talk to your boy friend?' he asked.

'It was my mother.'

A teacher was passing. Lewis put his hands in his pockets, to look like two friends strolling. 'Everything all right at home?'

'Yes.' Callie did not dare to say, Mind your own business. 'We're expecting a foal,' she said nervously, because they were turning into an empty corridor and it was safer to keep him talking. 'At least, Specs is. That's what we call her, because she's got white hair round her eyes, like spectacles.' She laughed uneasily.

Lewis did not say anything. When they reached a corner, he suddenly peeled off like a fighter plane and was gone. He did not seem so vicious this term. Perhaps he was growing out of it at last. Perhaps it was going to be a lucky year.

26

Two nights later, the telephone rang. Everyone in the house woke and sat up. It was two o'clock in the morning. The ringing in the hall sounded loudly through the still house, like disaster.

It was Mr Beckett.

'This is it, Colonel.' He was sputtering with rage. 'The horse was all over one corner of my winter wheat, and then right through my seedling fir trees, galloping as if the devil himself was behind. I took a pot shot at it. Said I would, didn't I? No, I didn't hit it, but I tell you, Colonel, I almost wish I had.'

It was Specs. The door of the foaling stable was wide open. Her hoofmarks led through the orchard and the open gateway, across the lane and on to Beckett's land.

The Colonel got into the car to go round to the other side of Beckett's farm. Steve and Dora and Callie were starting out on foot through the orchard when Steve stopped.

'Let's ride,' he said. 'If they chased her, she may be miles away.'

When they came out of the house, they had all heard the motorbike, screeching along the road into the downhill curve. They did not see the riders, but they were all sure who it was.

They took Cobby and Hero, and Dora rode the mule. It was a dark night. No moon, and a damp mist hanging over the ground, and on the trees like veils. They could not follow the mare's tracks.

They rode round the edges of Beckett's arable land, and

along a cart track between his cow pastures. Ahead of them, they saw the Colonel's lights on the road and went to join him.

'Better go home,' he said. 'We'll try in the morning.'

They went back into the fields, but they did not go home. They kept riding about in circles, farther afield, covering the land. If Specs heard or smelled the horses, she might come to them.

When the first line of light began to creep along the edge of the far hills, they were all exhausted, and the mule was falling into every rut and over every stone, even those that were not there. Callie was cold and Hero was bored. Every time they made a turn away from home, he would fight to turn back. Steve and the Cobbler rode ahead, picking their way between the low bushes scattered over a fallow field. They were a long way from home. Callie was not even sure where they were.

Halfway across the field, Cobby suddenly raised his head, his small pointed ears tightly forward. He stopped. Steve pushed him on, but he stopped again, head up, all his senses alert.

'He's heard something,' said Steve, 'or got a scent.'

'Probably a field of oats,' Dora said.

'Let's see where he'll go.'

Steve dropped the reins and sent him forward. Cobby broke into a jog. They went through a gap in the hedge and over a stubble field. At the far end, a plank bridge took them over a deep dry ditch. The mule hesitated, distrusting the bridge. Dora slapped him with the flat of her hand, and he was just scrambling across when Cobby stopped again and backed, almost knocking Willy into the ditch.

He switched off to the side, and as they followed the edge of the ditch, they saw the dark shape of the mare.

Callie held the horses, while Steve and Dora jumped down

to Specs. The foal had been born. It had been born still wrapped in the thin sac of membrane which had protected it for so long, floating inside its mother. Jammed in the ditch, weak and exhausted, the mare could not turn and rip the sac with her teeth, and the foal was suffocating, drowning in the fluid.

'Just in time.'

Steve freed the small wet head. They could not tell if it was alive or dead. Dora had once seen a man fished out of the river and saved by mouth-to-mouth breathing. She took the foal's head and breathed steadily into its nose, until its lungs moved and the foal began to breathe life of its own.

When they showed her her wet black colt, poor old Specs was too weak to lick it. She bumped it with her grey whiskery nose, and then dropped back her head.

Her eyes were glazed and dull. She looked as if she would die.

Steve rode across the field, and followed the road to the nearest house, where he astonished a sleeping family with a demand for blankets for a dying mare and her new-born foal.

When it was light, the Colonel came with a break-down lorry and a canvas sling. Somehow they got Specs out of the ditch and on to her feet. The Colonel and Steve and the two men from the garage pulled and pushed and half carried her up the ramp into the horse box. Callie sat on the floor in front with her arms round the struggling, long-legged foal.

As soon as he was in the stable with his mother, he pushed his face against the exhausted mare and tried to suck, but there was no milk for him.

The vet came three times that day, and gave Specs injections, but she had been infected from the difficult birth, and in the evening, he said, 'She hasn't got much chance. You'd better try and find a foster mother.'

'We're going to raise him by hand.' Callie pulled the colt away from his mother and pushed the bottle of milk into his soft mouth.

Slugger's wife had found a feeding bottle that had been used for one of her grandchildren, and they fed the colt with milk from the old man's goat. It had to be fed little and often, the way a mare feeds her foal, wandering away from it before it can take too much.

'Never rear it,' Slugger droned. 'You know what they say: Lose a mare, lose a foal.'

'What about cows? They take the calf away at once and feed it by hand, don't they?'

The Colonel borrowed a special calf feeding pail from Mr Beckett, who had calmed down when they explained that last night was not their fault, but the colt much preferred Slugger's grandchild's bottle.

He was always hungry. It seemed to be always time to feed him. At almost any hour of the day or night, you could find the Colonel or Anna or Steve or Dora or Callie or Toby tipping the bottle of goat's milk down to the soft, demanding nose, the long legs braced, tail quivering, blue eyes bulging with greed. They took it in turn to set their alarm clocks and go down in the night to the stable where Specs lay in the straw, licking anxiously at her foal, her white-rimmed eyes full of the trouble she could not understand. The fever had gone into her feet, and she would not stand.

But the colt would not give up. He was full of life and bounce, and he gave his mother no peace.

'Shouldn't we take him away from her?' Dora was trying to get Specs to eat, holding the food in her hand. The mare would nibble a bit, then turn her head away. 'She isn't getting any better.'

'But she's alive.' The Colonel would never give up his stubborn hope of life for his animals. 'She's alive because she's got a colt. Take him away, and you take away her will to hang on.'

The colt was called Folly, as Callie had planned. Cobbler's Folly, Steve called him, since it was Cobbler's Dream who had found him.

Callie hated being away from him at school.

'Had your foal yet?' Lewis asked quite affably.

'Yes. A colt.'

He raised his thick eyebrows, which met in the middle of his nose, so that his whole brow furrowed when he moved them.

'Mother and child doing well?'

He lowered the brows. With those dull eyes and that hanging mouth, you could not tell how much he was hiding. It *must* have been him and the Toad who chased our poor Specs. But there was no way to prove it.

'The colt is lovely,' Callie said. 'But the poor old mother nearly died.'

'Oh well,' said the Louse. 'We all come to it.'

Callie did not tell him that because the lovely colt had kept bothering Specs to get up and feed him, the milk had begun to come at last, and the fever left her. She did not tell him about the miracle. He would not understand things like that.

Some time after that, Lewis stopped coming to school.

Steve had to go back to the hospital for a final X-ray. While he was there, one of the nurses, the one who had written, 'Love always Susie' on his plaster cast, gave him some interesting news.

Two patients had come in with food poisoning, which was traced to a tin of contaminated meat found on the rubbish heap at the Pinecrest Hotel, where they were staying.

The hotel had been closed down and the owners had gone away.

The old man came back in the spring. When they told him about Specs, he nodded and sucked his loose false teeth and did not say anything.

Specs and her colt belonged to him, of course. Callie went sadly out to the field. Folly left the other horses and came to her at once. He still liked people best, because they had first cared for him.

He put his inquiring nose into her hand. She let him lick the salt of her skin, and then flung her arms round his neck and wept into his growing mane. The colt put his head down to graze, to get rid of her, and moved away.

When Steve came to the gate, Callie was sitting in the grass, tearing daisies to pieces.

'Stop sulking,' he said. 'He's gone.'

Callie looked up and saw Steve through a mist of sun and tears.

'The old man has moved into his daughter's flat. We're keeping Specs and Folly.'